CANCELLED

HAND OVER MIND

By Marc Lovell

HAND OVER MIND

MARC LOVELL

PUBLISHED FOR THE CRIME CLUB BY

DOUBLEDAY & COMPANY, INC.

GARDEN CITY, NEW YORK

1979

All of the characters in this book
are fictitious, and any resemblance
to actual persons, living or dead,
is purely coincidental.

Library of Congress Cataloging in Publication Data

Lovell, Marc.
  Hand over mind.

  I. Title.
PZ4.L89913Han 1979 [PR6062.0853] 823
ISBN: 0-385-15639-1
Library of Congress Catalog Card Number 79-7669

HAND OVER MIND

PROLOGUE

The houses are identical. Sitting fifty feet apart, side by side, they are long and low and luxurious, with extensive use of fieldstone and hardwood. The roofing is imported slate. The shared forecourt is cobbled. In the one long open-fronted garage that connects the houses are matching grey Cadillacs and matching blue pickup trucks.

To round out the picture satisfyingly, the two men now pacing the forecourt together ought to be twins. Instead, the brothers Scott are quite unalike, except for height and bulk.

Harry, at thirty-five the older by a year, is fresh-faced with fair hair. His features look to be on the point of relaxing around a smile; they have that openness, honesty, charm. He has a sloppy way of moving his body.

Jack Scott is what used to be called dashing. He is dark, handsome and restive, with compelling eyes and a wry grin that appears as frequently and briefly as his frowns, nods, and winks: the busy face of a busy-minded man.

On this October afternoon the Scott brothers are wearing heavy topcoats in protection against the Ontario cold. The sun is mistily timid. In the sky is a look of snow. The trees that surround the property, though at a respectable distance, are sadly dropping their last, Indian summer leaves, surrendering before the inevitable white massacre.

Harry and Jack Scott end their pacing by the low wall that rims the forecourt. Harry sits on it; Jack uses it as a footrest. The men talk on, their breath forming clouds.

The subject is business, the latest step in the operation of this farm, a two-hundred-thousand-acre spread known as the O'Neal place.

The brothers are successful because they rarely agree, but between pulling and dragging they manage to reach the right position. Harry is the farmer—he went to agricultural college—and Jack the organiser—he has a degree in business administration.

Now, as usual, Jack is saying what has to be done and Harry is explaining why it can't. They talk easily. Whereas these exchanges used to be heated, nowadays they are calm, for there is less at stake: the farm is well established, for one thing, and for another a good half of it is parcelled off to tenants and sharecroppers.

The Scotts are satisfied. Jack has more time for his golf and other business enterprises, Harry has no need to pretend that he isn't basically lazy.

"You just don't understand," Harry is saying, "that soil has its limits."

"Sure I understand. I should—you've told me enough times. It needs a sabbatical every once in a while."

"Right. If not strictly every seven years."

Jack says, "So you want to let the west two thousand lie fallow. Fallow and useless."

"Can't be helped. That piece of land needs a rest."

The brothers look toward the west. They fall silent. Jack lights a cigarette, Harry lets his gaze slowly lower from the trees to the ground. The silence continues.

Harry is the first to break it. He says, as if giving voice to a thought, "Soon it'll be a year."

Jack blinks. "What?"

Looking confused, Harry gets up. "Sorry."

Jack smiles and gives his brother a light punch on the shoulder. He says, "Nothing to be sorry about."

"Sure."

"You're not reminding me of anything that wasn't there in the first place."

Again Harry says, "Sure."

They begin to walk toward the pair of houses. Jack asks, "What brought it to your mind anyway?"

"The weather."

"It was a bit milder than this, I think."

"Pretty much the same," Harry says. "Except for slush."

The pause that follows has a mutual message: end of subject. Their voices are different for:

"Will it snow, Harry? What d'you think?"

"She's trying but she won't make it."

"I'll let 'em know at the club they can plan on playing tomorrow. No snow. The expert has pronounced judgement."

They laugh.

Between the houses the men separate with a casual "See you later." Jack goes to one of the Cadillacs, gets in and drives off. After watching him out of sight, Harry takes a shotgun from the front of his blue pickup, puts it into the break position and carries it barrel down over his arm. He goes to the house on the left, to its back door.

The kitchen is gleamingly modern. It is unsuited to the stout middle-aged woman working there, with her broad Nordic face and greying hair drawn back into an old-fashioned bun.

She asks, "Did you get me a rabbit, Mr. Harry?"

"Didn't see a thing."

"And Mr. Jack? Will he be in for supper?"

"Guess so. In fact, yes, as he didn't say otherwise."

"I'm fixing a roast."

Pausing by an interior doorway, Harry says with a smile, "Mrs. Maynard, we've had a roast on Thursdays for as long as I've known you."

"And for a good few years before that," the woman says, as though she were admitting to an achievement. "You ask Mrs. Scott."

"And before she was born?"

"Surely. That's what Mrs. O'Neal wanted, and that's what Mrs. O'Neal got."

Harry nods and goes on. He enters the vast living room, its decor professional but kept within reason. An imitation log fire emits a flickering glow.

A broad, carpeted ramp in one corner takes Harry down to a door. Through that is a basement recreation room—pool table, dart board, weight-lifting equipment.

Harry puts the shotgun in a glass-fronted gun cupboard, which he locks, pocketing the key. After taking off his coat and tossing it on a chair, he goes back up the slope.

His wife is standing by the hearth. She is slim and graceful, stands well, lending elegance to her jeans and sweater. She has long straight blond hair. Her face, attractive reaching for beautiful, is solemn. There are dark shadows under her eyes, themselves blue and wary and restless.

She says, "I thought I heard you come in."

Harry goes to her and kisses her cheek. "Did you have a nap?"

Elaine Scott shakes her head, the hair swinging. "Couldn't. I'll sleep all the better tonight."

"Of course you will. It's best not to fool with sleeping pills. I don't like drugs."

Elaine says, "Did I hear you talking to Jack outside?"

Harry nods. "Be back later. He's gone into town. His secretary has some papers for him to sign."

"Busy Jack," Elaine says. Her voice, as all along, is pale and tired, a monotone.

"Any calls?"

"No. Oh yes. Haig Wilson. He wanted us for dinner on

the twenty-sixth of October. I said could we leave it open.
He said okay."

Harry looks at his wife. "You don't want to go?"

"I'll see. I don't think so."

After nodding slowly, Harry Scott says, "I wish you'd let
me have Henry come out and check you over again. Or we
could try another doctor."

"I'm fine, dear," Elaine says, her voice gaining strength,
her shoulders straightening. "It's the time of year."

"Oh?"

"You know. The fall. Autumn's like twilight. A closing.
There's something poignant about it." She turns to the mantelshelf and plays at rearranging objects. "Don't worry
about me, Harry."

"Okay. But I don't want you turning into a recluse."

"I won't."

"You haven't been yourself these past few weeks. Longer."

Elaine Scott turns. "Maybe we will go Saturday."

"Whatever you like."

"Listen. What were you and Jack talking about?"

Harry tells her and they go over the matter of the west
two thousand. Elaine's eyes become more restless. Once she
nods instead of shaking her head. Presently she says:

"You're the farmer, dear. You know best."

"Let's hope so."

With a touch on her husband's arm, Elaine moves away.
"Things to do. See you."

Alone, Harry makes himself comfortable in a leather armchair that bears the marks of time and is despised by the
rest of the furniture. He fusses with a pipe, gets it going, set-
tles to reading an historical novel.

Time passes.

Harry puts down pipe and book. Getting up, he yawns
and stretches. For a while he stands by the picture window,

looking out. He leaves the room via an open arch and goes along a passage to the sleeping quarters. At the door of his wife's bedroom he listens. It's quiet inside. He taps lightly. Elaine might be napping. Or she could be at work: she writes verse.

Getting no answer, Harry opens the door softly. Elaine is on the davenport, sitting hunched forward. A pad on her knee, she is writing; and swiftly, her hand moving at speed over the page.

Harry says, "Honey?"

Elaine Scott neither answers nor looks up.

Puzzled at this unusual degree of concentration, Harry goes inside and over to the davenport. "Elaine?" he says, and touches his wife's shoulder. There is still no response.

Harry Scott sinks to one knee. He looks up into Elaine's down-tilted face. Her eyes are half closed, her features are rigid, her breathing is as deep as a sleeper's.

Harry shakes his wife gently. She neither speaks nor takes her gaze from the pad. Her hand goes busily on—writing, writing, writing.

ONE

The frame house in a quiet Toronto suburb had two functions. The lower level was the home of the Ontario Society for Psychical Research; upstairs was the home of that organisation's president, Andrew Bailey.

The white house with blue trim was so mundane that visitors to OSPR were often offended. They expected something along the Gothic line, or barred windows, or at least a setting not so middle class and respectable. The lack of drama was a distinct disappointment. The neighbours had long since stopped being intrigued, and their children had given up expecting howls, screams in the night, and apparitions.

If others were disillusioned, the Ontario Society for Psychical Research was satisfied. It preferred being either ignored or placidly accepted. Its professional path, it knew, was a narrow one which had scorn on one side and outright hostility on the other. Progress wasn't helped by their attention, or by the loud gushing of approval from the believers, who pushed and pulled along the path.

OSPR wanted to maintain the dignity it had fought for and well deserved. It avoided publicity and went on discreetly with its job of exploring man's last frontier.

The society had a Board of Governors and three paid, full-time employees. Funds came in the form of bequests, gifts, a subsidy from the provincial government, grants from foundations and universities. It was a thriving organisation.

There were regular meetings of members, lectures, an advice service, a library open to all, the publication of a quarterly journal, and hundreds of volunteers to call on for field work.

Andrew Bailey was eminently suited to be the head of OSPR's active work force. A fence sitter, he said neither yea nor nay to the supernatural, only maybe. He kept his mind so open that at times he thought his position to be untenable, feeling that he should fall one side or the other off the fence. But he couldn't bring himself to do it. He was like that. He had to be sure.

At forty-two, widower Andrew Bailey was tall and athletic. His face was also strong, with a square jaw, a forceful nose and a firm mouth. His dark hair, greying at the temples, added an extra touch of vibrancy with its wave and density.

One sunny October morning, wearing flannels, tweed jacket and a polo-neck sweater, Andrew came downstairs to the reception area. Lined with books, it held easy chairs as well as the desk of Ann Goodwin, receptionist and secretary, though Andrew preferred to call her his assistant.

A greater preference for Andrew would have been to call her Mrs. Bailey. Ann often felt the same, but that was usually during the times when Andrew was thinking in the other direction, having decided yet again that their differences were unsurmountable. In the past year an engagement ring had gone back and forth several times.

Andrew was heading across the lobby, toward his office, when he heard a noise. Changing directions, he went into the laboratory. It was bright from the fluorescent lighting. A muffled voice called, "Hi, Chief. Be with you in a minute. Take a pew."

What Andrew sat on was, in fact, a church pew. It wasn't the large room's only oddity, in addition to the normal equipment of research quarters, from sinks to Bunsen burners.

A coffin lid was fixed to the ceiling. A corner held a male dummy in evening dress and on roller skates. There were tombstones made of papier-mâché. A medium's cabinet lay on its side. The walls held photostats of ancient recipes for making gold, posters that announced spiritualist meetings, Tarot cards, countless photographs of people and places, various lengths of cheesecloth and a few toy trumpets. Scattered around the benches and tables, in every possible size, were cameras and tape recorders.

From behind a bank of speakers appeared John Bright. The lab technician was thirty years old, short, and tubby. His prematurely thinning hair he wore long at the back; it looked like a slipped wig. He had a chunky, pleasant face that rarely lacked a smile.

John Bright was perfect for his role as a professional exposer of frauds. He had been an insurance investigator, assistant to a stage magician, was an expert mechanic, a first-rate photographer, and had a wary attitude to most aspects of life. John Bright was a happy cynic.

Andrew asked, "Been working on that tape?"

"Right, Chief. Boring myself stiff. It's ready when you are."

"Ring up the curtain."

"But it'll be far simpler if I explain," John Bright said. "Save you wasting your time. It's an easy one. And no hanky-panky."

"Not even good old landlord harassment?"

"No good old anything."

Two days before, a woman had asked OSPR to investigate the presence of ghost voices. They had started to echo around the house that she had been renting for years. At the house, while Andrew kept the woman busy in the garden—

no one being above suspicion in these affairs—John Bright
had placed his recorders in whatever hiding places he could
find. He had returned to the house the previous night to
pick up his equipment.

"The lady recently bought her first hi-fi record player," he
said now. "She sometimes forgets to switch it off when the
last record's finished. Can you guess the rest?"

"I'm warm. But you tell me."

"As often happens, the set faintly picks up radio signals."

"Some ghost."

"My tapes are full of landing instructions from the air-
port. A laugh a minute."

Andrew nodded. As always at moments like this, he was
experiencing a curious feeling which he knew was a mingling of disappointment and relief.

John Bright said, "But it must've been pretty eerie for the
old girl, these voices mumbling what to her was gibberish."

"Sure. In fact, since you say this happens often, it might
be an idea to write it up for the *Journal*."

"Fine. Could save a few nervous breakdowns."

"And listen," Andrew said. "Try not to crow about the
case to Ann. She had high hopes for this one."

John Bright grinned. "I'll do my best, Chief."

They talked of other matters until Andrew heard the front
door close. He went out to the lobby. Ann Goodwin was
hanging up her topcoat.

The third OSPR employee, in her mid-twenties, was a
strikingly pretty girl. She had black hair to her shoulders
and a shapely figure. Her eyes were particularly engaging:
large and dark, soulful and calm.

Ann was a believer. With Andrew being a middle-of-the-
road man and John Bright being an outright heretic, Ann
completed the balance.

It was that belief in the supernatural, however, like a

difference in religious faith, that kept Ann and Andrew from finalising their relationship. Ann was incapable of taking a light view. She was fervent and dedicated. Ghost jokes turned her icy and she couldn't debate objectively when she met a scoffer.

Ann had all the avidity of a convert but was saved from being the nuisance that that implies by having a sense of humour.

Andrew went to her and they kissed briefly. "You look great," Andrew said. "Love that dress."

"What, this brand-new thing that cost the earth?" Ann said. Then she smiled. "Thanks."

Andrew bowed. He asked, "By the way, are we engaged at the moment? I've forgotten."

Ann lifted a ringless left hand as she glanced toward the laboratory. Her smile holding, she asked, "Did John come up with anything on his tapes?"

"I guess you mean that new case."

"Well, yes. Naturally."

Andrew scratched the hair above his ear, cleared his throat. "As a matter of fact . . ." he began.

Ann said, "Oh." She listened straight-faced to Andrew's recounting of the reason for the strange voices. "I think I'll avoid John this morning."

"Cheer up, sweet. Hearing people mumbling was a bit cracked in the first place."

"Do you think so?" Ann asked coolly. "I'm not sure that I agree with you there."

"Anyway," Andrew hurried on, "let's think about other voices. I mean the Gilbert and Sullivan show tonight. If we're going I'd better call in and reserve seats."

Ann began, "As a matter of fact . . ."

"Oh," Andrew said. "Your parents?"

"They'd like me to stay home and make up a fourth. But I don't know. The show sounds better."

"Think about it."

"Will do."

Andrew went into his office. At the desk he telephoned the woman with the hi-fi and explained the nature of her haunting. She was volubly grateful and, with gentle prompting, agreed to send a donation to the society.

Andrew started on his mail. He was still reading when the intercom buzzed. He clicked the switch. Ann said, "Mr. Bailey, there's a Mr. Harold Scott here to see you."

Ann was excited. The visitor had explained his reasons for wanting an interview with the head of OSPR. It sounded like a perfect example of automatic writing to Ann, who had never before come close to the phenomenon, except in research papers.

Ann Goodwin had been preoccupied with the paranormal ever since puberty. At that time there had been considerable poltergeist activity in her home. Of their own accord, it seemed, objects were thrown about, the furniture moved, cushions emptied, all without apparent pattern or malice toward any particular person.

The sole constant was that the prankish mayhem took place only when Ann was in the vicinity. She, in any case, was the prime suspect. Teen-agers moving into adulthood are almost always cited as the innocent corporal contacts of poltergeists, if not their guilty impersonators.

The investigation by the Ontario Society for Psychical Research, then newly founded, was inconclusive. Ann was (a) causing the disturbances for some reason of her own, was (b) causing them but not aware of doing so, suffering periods of fugue due to her changing body and emotions, or

(c) the phenomena were genuine. Before the investigation could intensify, the poltergeist activity faded away.

There had been nothing of that nature since for Ann. But there had been other oddities which had kept her to her conviction that she was psychic, one of the chosen. Often, if she had a strong rapport with a person, she knew what he was going to say before he said it. She listened to conversations that she knew she had heard before somewhere, or visited a house and knew she had been in it at some previous time, though not physically, or met someone and knew at once if they were going to be friends.

While Ann was aware that thousands of other people had these same sensations, she felt that those were due to coincidence or imagination; only a few, the gifted, had experiences as strong and detailed and absolute as her own. The fact that those thousands of others felt the same she ignored.

Ann looked at the closed door of Andrew's office, her stare trying to melt wood. She wondered how unethical it would be to listen at the keyhole.

The intercom buzzed. Ann swung around fast and stabbed down the switch. Andrew said, "Would you come in with your pad, please, Miss Goodwin. I want you to hear this and take notes."

Two minutes later Ann was sitting at the desk with Andrew and Harry Scott. The latter was playing restlessly with an unlit pipe. Andrew was lighting a fresh cigarette from the stub of an old one, which, Ann knew with pleasure, was a sure sign that he was intrigued. She reached for a cigarette herself.

"All right, Mr. Scott," Andrew said. "Please go on. Your wife was writing and seemed to be in a trance."

"A trance, yes. That's the only way I can describe it. But I've never seen one before, so I wouldn't know."

"What did you do?"

"I called Mrs. Maynard. She's our live-in help. She said best not to disturb Elaine. Her condition could be like sleep-walking or something. So we just sat there and watched her." Harry Scott shrugged helplessly.

Andrew asked, "How long did the trance last?"

"Another five, ten minutes. And the writing never paused. Next my wife sort of drooped, gave a deep sigh, and went into what looked like a normal sleep. When she woke up an hour later she was her usual self."

Andrew blew out smoke. "I suppose you told her what had been happening."

Harry Scott said, "Yes, and she admitted that the same thing had happened to her a couple of days before. I mean, she'd come out of a sleep to find pages of writing."

"But she hadn't told you about that."

"She was worried about it. She still is, though she tries to make out that it's unimportant. She doesn't like these trances any more than I do."

"There've been more, then?"

"Four more since the one I saw, which was a week ago. They happen about every other day."

Ann couldn't stop herself from butting in. She asked, "And Mrs. Scott always writes?"

"On the next trance she was reading a paper," the visitor said. "Her hand moved across it as if writing. The one after that, I put a pad on her lap and a pen in her hand. She's written in every trance but one."

"Those that you know of."

"Well, yes."

Andrew put out his cigarette. "All right now, Mr. Scott, let's get to the nature of that writing. I'd like you to describe it, please."

"A scribble is what it is," the visitor said, passing his pipe from one hand to the other. "You can only make out a word here and there. It's totally unlike my wife's usual writing, which is pretty nice. Anyway, my brother has a secretary who's fairly good with longhand, and she's managed to decipher ninety-five per cent of the scripts. The latest one she typed out. I've brought it with me."

"When the words have been deciphered," Andrew said, "can you then relate them to the originals?"

"Oh, sure. The stuff isn't in a code. It's simply plain bad, slurry writing."

Andrew asked, "What are these scripts about?"

Harry Scott spread his hands. "They're rambling, first-person narratives about what appear to be everyday doings, nothing definite happening, just sensations, emotions. Pretty vague altogether."

Ann, who had smiled at the mention of first person, managed this time not to ask the question that came to her, but she was pleased when Andrew spoke it for her, using the identical words she had chosen herself.

"Do the scripts have any names?"

"No, none."

"Not even the narrator's?"

"No names, Mr. Bailey."

Andrew shook a cigarette out of the pack on the desk. After lighting up, he said, "Let's have a few family details, Mr. Scott, if you don't mind, before we go any further."

For the next quarter hour Ann was busy making notes, which she would later type out for the folio that in her mind she had already entitled "The Scott Case."

Hard facts taken care of, Andrew asked, "What does your wife think of it all, Mr. Scott?"

"She refuses to discuss it," the visitor said. "On the other hand, she seems to me to be a little brighter after every session of writing."

"Her normal state isn't cheerful, you mean?"

"Well, she's been a bit off colour lately."

"And your own thoughts?"

Harry Scott rubbed the bowl of his pipe as though it were a worry bead or a magic lamp. "I'm concerned," he said. "I'd prefer to call in a doctor or a psychiatrist—if you'll pardon me for saying so. You see, I don't believe in the supernatural."

"I'm not sure that I do either."

"Oh? But I thought . . ."

"I'm an investigator, Mr. Scott. That's what OSPR is all about."

"I see."

"And I have a degree in psychology," Andrew said, smiling, "if that makes you feel any better."

Scott answered the smile quickly, as though with relief. "Yes, it does."

"Your brother, his secretary, and your housekeeper—what do they think about it?"

"Well, I don't know about Mrs. Maynard, but the others seem to think it's genuine. Jack, my brother, says it should be encouraged, even if only on account of the money."

"What money?"

"There's an old story, Jack says, that Moina O'Neal brought ten thousand golden sovereigns with her when she came to this country, and that they're still around somewhere."

"That's your wife's grandmother that you mentioned a minute ago."

"Right. She came to Canada from Ireland around the turn of the century."

"How does she fit into all this?" Andrew asked, though Ann could have told him, and was proved right when the visitor said:

"Everyone seems to be of the opinion that the writing is

connected with her, although, as I've said, there's no nam-
ing of names in the scripts. But she was a pretty strong character. It's a reasonable assumption."

"But you don't share it."

"I do not."

Andrew slowly turned his swivel chair to face the window
that looked out onto the long rear garden. To her annoyance, Ann found herself thinking what an impressive,
handsome picture he formed.

She turned to the visitor. "Did you keep the early scripts,
Mr. Scott?"

"I did. And the original of this one." He brought out an
envelope, which he put on the desk.

Andrew swung back. He said, "I take it, then, that you
are formally requesting the Ontario Society for Psychical
Research to investigate this matter?"

While Ann was wishing that Andrew wouldn't sound so
pompous on these occasions, Harry Scott was fumbling that
he supposed he was, he didn't know what else to do, it
would be something at least if he could be satisfied that the
cause was from outside his wife's own mind.

Andrew got up. "Very well, Mr. Scott. I'll think over what
you've told me, read through this transcription, and get in
touch with you later today. We'll discuss the next step
then."

Ann was reaching for the envelope before the two men
had left the office.

Another beautiful day. It ravishes the eye. What a
marvellous place to live. It's a pity I don't always realise
that and enjoy everything about me. Mostly, though, I
do. I love nature, the changing seasons, the excitement
of each new spring, the stages of life that are like
friendly inns on a long road. Every little sight and smell

and sound is a miracle. The birds and animals, a baby's laugh. The bouquet of new-mown hay and the orchard blossom, bread fresh from the oven and the church on a rainy morning. One of my hairs shining against black velvet, apples ripening on the window ledge, icicles, the way grass slowly gets to its feet again after it's been trodden on. There's so much. Even when he's late. As now. But work has to be done. Perhaps a new foal to be seen to. Young things are so gracious. We ought to have more of them around. They're so heavenly, they remind me of God, and I do believe in God, just as I do in being fair, which probably amounts to the same thing. It must be hard to be a saint. Harder to swallow all the fuss, the pomp and circumstance, that the saint gets when he's dead and that he turned his back on in life. It's not logical. All Saints' Day isn't far off. Last year it was a delight. We all had such fun. Best of all, I think, was the children's faces. That glow. The eyes. And the younger the better, naturally. Every morsel of the magic fades away as you grow up. Christmas becomes a mark on the calendar, or an excuse for parties and drinking. You have to see things in a different light when you're older. It's sad. Which we haven't to be because we have so many blessings. We have no right to sadness. What I must do is go to the kitchen and talk of serious matters, such as cookies. She's a winner at fun shapes. That gnome last year was a wild success. I might try some myself when she's out, on her day off, but I won't tell. That's her domain, after all, and fair enough. One should avoid shadows. I don't like shadows.

"Moina O'Neal came to Ontario as a widow," Ann was saying, reading from her typed notes. "She had her only child with her, the father of Mrs. Elaine Scott. Moina bought land and built up a farm almost singlehanded. She married again later, but that one ended in divorce. She died about twenty-five years ago, at the age of eighty-six."

Andrew said, "To quote her grandson-in-law, a pretty strong character." He was sitting on a corner of Ann's desk. John Bright leaned on a nearby bookcase.

Ann went on, "Her son let the farm get run down, but the Scott brothers worked it back into shape, after Harry had married Elaine. Jack Scott has an office in Hamlyn Creek, five miles away. He's a dabbler, sells crop insurance and so forth. The township is thirty miles from here. Harry and Elaine have no children. That's her decision. She believes the world today is not a fit place in which to raise a family."

"Principles yet," John Bright said.

Andrew: "Some of old Moina in there, I'd say." He put a light to his cigarette. "Anything else, Ann?"

"No, that's the lot."

Andrew looked at John Bright. "Well, you've read the transcript of Elaine Scott's writing, and you've heard the details. What d'you think of it?"

"Ill," the lab technician said airily. "The lady should be having couch treatment."

Ann said, "Honestly, John!"

"Now, children," Andrew put in. "Let's not start on the old ping-pong game that nobody wins." He thought it a pity he had to cut them off: Ann looked particularly beautiful when she was riled.

"It'll be as easy as the last case," John Bright said. "If she isn't cuckoo, she's faking it."

Ann asked, "Why?"

"Dozens of reasons. You know that as well as I do. There's a motive for everything."

Andrew stubbed out the half-smoked cigarette. His

mouth was foul from the morning's excess smoking. He asked, "And what do you think of it, Ann?"

She folded her arms firmly. "Well, the signs point toward a genuine case of automatic writing. That is, Elaine Scott being under the control of another mind."

"Which," the lab man said, "could be a living mind."

Ann nodded. "That's a remote possibility, yes. I try to be reasonable about these things. But most likely Elaine's control is no longer among the corporal living."

"Worth an investigation?" Andrew asked, sharing his glance.

The other two said in unison, "Yes." And John Bright added, "What do you think about it, Chief?"

Andrew scratched the hair above his ear. "I'm intrigued," he said. "More so than I would be usually." He got off the desk, moved to the other corner, sat again. "Ann, an academic question. What is automatic writing?"

"In psychology, it's like a Freudian slip. It's done without conscious intent. Sort of doodling."

"In parapsychology?"

Ann said, "It's a form of discarnate agency. As the medium sitting in séance produces verbal messages from the dead, so does the automatic writer produce written messages. The phenomenon is extremely well documented. You've heard of Patience Worth, of course."

"I think so, yes."

Ann got up and crossed to a bank of books. With unerring aim she took out a volume, which she brought back to the desk. "This is only one of many on the case. It was written by Dr. Prince of the Boston Society for Psychical Research."

Andrew listened carefully, John Bright restlessly, while Ann talked of a Mrs. Curran of St. Louis, Missouri, who in 1913 began producing written communications from someone who called herself Patience Worth, who had lived in

England in the late seventeenth century, who had gone to the New World, who had been killed there by Indians.

"Patience was a sharp-tongued woman with a strong will," Ann said. "She didn't limit herself to chitchat. She began to dictate stories and other works. The final output was something like three million words."

"You're kidding," John Bright said.

"Not at all. A lot of the stuff was actually published commercially, for general sale, and by reputable New York houses. The case is widely accepted as genuine. Mrs. Curran was an ill-educated woman who couldn't of her own accord have produced those novels, prayers, poems, and so forth."

John Bright looked at the ceiling to murmur, "I wonder who got the royalties?"

Andrew tapped the volume. "I'll read up on the case."

"Do, Andrew. It's fascinating."

"And I know of Walter Franklin Prince. A sound reputation for exhaustive investigation."

Ann sat in her chair. "Andrew," she said, "why are you especially intrigued with this Scott affair?"

"Well, I've been toying with a theory lately. If I get it worked out, I'll do a piece on it for the *Journal*. It has to do with that fledgling science sociobiology."

Ann said, "I'm not sure that I know what it is."

The lab technician moved from the shelves, as if making a show of leaving the paranormal behind him. "Now that's really fascinating," he said. "It supposes that our behaviour is given to us through the genes, just as our physical characteristics are."

"That's foolish," Ann said.

"Most psychologists scream the same thing, but there's definitely something in it. Environment has a big part to play in behaviour, of course, but so do the genes."

"Are you telling me that if my father were a bad-tempered cuss I'd tend to be the same?"

"Something like that, though not so flippant."

"My dear John," Ann said sweetly, "you invented flippancy around here."

Andrew said, "Automatic writing is a degree of reincarnation, assuming that we accept it as a communication from the dead. The writer, if only for short periods, becomes that person from the past. Agreed?"

Ann said, "Agreed."

Andrew again tapped the book on the desk. "Patience Worth could, for the sake of argument, have been a forebear of her automatist, Mrs. Curran. Which brings us to my theory."

John Bright asked, "Sociobiology?"

"Exactly. Let's put it this way. If brown eyes, say, can be passed on over the generations, if also inheritable are tendencies to be brave or romantic or misanthropic or a thousand things else, why couldn't the genes pass on other information? I mean memory. The Currans could inherit the memories of the Worths, though be unaware of it except under very special circumstances, perhaps some emotional turmoil."

"There'd be nothing at all supernatural about it," the lab man said, nodding slowly. "Perfectly biological and beautifully scientific."

"So why," Ann asked, "can't we all dip into these memories of our ancestors? If not at will, during the emotional turmoil or what have you."

Andrew said, "I haven't worked it out fully, not by a long way. I'm still biting at the edges. But it could be that the descendant, the Curran, has to be particularly sensitive, for one thing. For another, she has to be in a trance state in order to get to that area of her mind that stores the information. For a third, perhaps she needs to be a strong throwback, greatly like the forebear both physically and mentally."

Still nodding, John Bright said, "I like it. It's almost got both feet on the ground."

Andrew went on, "This could, in fact, be the answer we've all been looking for to explain the usual process of communication with the dead—spiritualism."

Ann sat taller. "Yes?"

"There's so much that science has been unable to disprove, always falling back on the excuse of coincidence when it can't show fakery."

Ann: "Precisely."

"The medium, you mean," John Bright said, "has the needed attributes to get into that hidden mind-area of the sitters at the séance. Sure. It's neat."

"Oh," Ann said. "You're still talking about sociobiology."

"Right."

"So how about your medium's sitters who aren't descendants of the dead communicants, no blood connections—friends, wives?"

Andrew nodded. "Okay, I should've said *part* of the answer."

Ann said, "I'm on the side of the shrinks. I think your sociobiology is nonsense, in normal psychology as well as the other variety."

"This is worth considering, Ann."

The secretary took up a piece of paper and began to roll it into her typewriter. "If you men of science will excuse me, I have a million letters to write."

As Andrew went into his office to telephone Harry Scott, he had a premonition. It took the form of a picture. He saw himself quite clearly going alone to see Gilbert and Sullivan.

TWO

Late the following afternoon Andrew was driving out of the city in his Ford. Sparkling sunshine made him put on sunglasses. The highway was dense with traffic, the start of the day's exodus, which made Andrew glad he wasn't a commuter. Yet he was also glad to be here now, taking this break from routine.

Yesterday he had spent half an hour on the telephone to Harry Scott. The result, after getting an okay from contactable members of the Board of Governors, was that Andrew was going to stay at the O'Neal farm while he investigated the purported automatic writing of Elaine Scott.

He would not, however, be a guest in the Scott home. That, Andrew felt, would be an imposition on them and a restriction on himself. His suggestion that he take a room in Hamlyn Creek had been bettered by Harry Scott, who had said:

"There's the old O'Neal house, five hundred yards back of us. We've used it before for guests, so it's quite livable."

"Sounds perfect," Andrew had said, and meant it.

"I'll only need to plug in some of the kitchen equipment and get the oil furnace going. You can eat with us whenever you feel like it, fix your own food, or go to town."

Andrew smiled as he left the last suburb and swung onto the highway. He was looking forward to staying in the home of Moina O'Neal. All in all, in fact, he was keen about the whole investigation.

Andrew had come to his post with OSPR after a series of unrelated jobs that followed his graduation from McGill. He had done social work, been a probation officer, gone from constable to detective with the Toronto force, taught at a private school, been an administrator at an Eskimo village in the Northwest Territories and principal of a home for retarded children.

Andrew's interest in the parapsychological had come from his wife. Often she had had dreams which came true, or partly true, or could be so interpreted. Andrew's view, though not derisive, was that coincidence was responsible. She begged him to quit the police force the week before three fellow officers were killed in a shoot-out with bank robbers. His view: intuition. She told him of a dream in which his application for the post at the private school had been successful, and that news of this had arrived in a blue envelope; which was what happened. Andrew had no view to offer.

His wife's most potent experience of foreknowledge was her last. One night when they were about to leave for the movies she said she was afraid to go because she kept hearing a fire truck. Andrew went alone. Part way through the show a message was flashed on the screen: Andrew Bailey was wanted out front. There, a policeman waited with the news that Andrew's house had caught on fire and his wife, escaping to an upper room, had died of suffocation.

Andrew went to the Northwest Territories. When grief suffered its inevitable loss of strength, he began to send away for books on psychic phenomena. Also he corresponded with the Ontario Society for Psychical Research, and with members conducted long-distance experiments in extrasensory perception. He ran similar tests with his Eskimo friends, whom he discovered to be particularly adept at thought communication.

To Andrew's relief he found that he was able to accept
ESP as fact, as had most of the scientific world. But he
couldn't accept any other facet of psychology beyond the
normal. He continued to argue with the scoffers and scoff at
the arguers. To both sides he said the same thing: Prove it.

Back in the Toronto area, working at the home for retarded children, Andrew became more closely connected
with OSPR, then became an authority on what had changed
from a hobby to a ghost which haunted him constantly and
which he was determined to either exorcise or bring to
stronger life. When the society's old president retired, Andrew, his willingness to have his house used as headquarters
lobbying for him, was voted by the Board into the vacant
post. His personal haunting went on.

It was dusk when Andrew drove through Hamlyn Creek.
The core of the village was one long street of businesses.
Lights were on and trade was brisk. That the area was in a
financial upper bracket showed in the size and type of store,
the number of banks, the youth of the vehicles lining the
kerbs.

Following the directions given him over the telephone,
Andrew drove along a series of dirt roads. At last he turned
through a gateway guarded by a small frame house. The private lane was hard-topped. It led into trees, out again, and
onto a forecourt.

Andrew stopped. He was still sitting in the car, admiring
the pair of houses, when from the one on the right a man
came striding. He saw the Ford and came across, asking,
"Mr. Bailey?"

Andrew got out. "Yes. And you must be Jack Scott."

They shook hands. "Nice to meet you, Mr. Bailey. How
d'you like it out here in the wilds?"

Andrew laughed. "I've been in wilder."

They chatted casually, lit cigarettes, were mild with one another in that way that strong personalities have when meeting for the first time, as if each wants to hold himself back for a surprise attack.

Andrew formed the impression that Jack Scott was a private person, hard to get to know; that he was sensitive about being taken for a slow-thinking farmer; and that he was easily bored—at least one part of his body was in constant movement.

Andrew said, "You don't look a bit like your brother, Mr. Scott."

"Like father like son, like mother like son. That's us. And talking of Harry, let's go in, eh?"

They went into the kitchen of the house on the left, where a woman introduced as Mrs. Maynard took their coats. From her Andrew thought he sensed a veiled antagonism.

Within minutes Andrew was sitting in a living room, holding a whiskey and soda, listening to the slim, blond Elaine Scott apologise for the lack of formality.

"For some reason," she said, "country people never use their front doors. I don't know why they bother to make them."

"It's fine with me," Andrew said. "I like the friendliness."

Beside him on the couch, Elaine Scott smiled. "Maybe the United Nations should put a ban on front doors."

"There's a thought."

Harry Scott, standing with his brother by the hearth, said, "By the way, Mr. Bailey, we're going out for dinner soon. I'm afraid you'll have to postpone your preliminary talk with my wife until tomorrow."

"No hurry about that."

Jack Scott said, "Good for you, Elaine. Glad you changed your mind. It'll do you good to get out."

"Yes."

Scott went on to talk about the local social scene, his tone lightly condescending.

Andrew looked covertly at the woman, who was gazing into her sherry—a token drink with a mere half inch of liquid in the glass. He noted the tired nervousness, the marks of strain that spoiled her prettiness, and the way she had of holding herself protectively together, legs neat, elbows close in, free hand near her throat. He also sensed that, the niceties of meeting having been observed, she was withdrawing into herself.

Her brother-in-law went toward a bar at one side of the room. "Anyone for seconds?"

The others declined. Harry Scott put a match to his pipe and between puffs said, "Any idea how long . . . this investigation . . . is going to take . . . Mr. Bailey?"

"No, I don't," Andrew said. "Sorry." It seemed to him that everyone was being particular about the use of titles, rather than the quick shift to first names that was common nowadays. That suited him fine. Best to keep things cool and efficient.

"Progress," he added, "will depend on you, Mrs. Scott."

She went on gazing into her glass. Her husband said, "Yes, of course, naturally."

Jack Scott finished his whiskey and excused himself to go and get changed. Harry said, after clearing his throat, "Mr. Bailey, my wife did some more writing today, didn't you, honey?"

Elaine Scott gave a faint nod. Andrew said, "Too bad I didn't get here earlier."

"I took it to town and it's being typed out by Rennie Bates, Jack's secretary. She'll bring you a copy later. The other transcripts are here as well, with the originals. Also there's all Moina O'Neal's papers, which you might find interesting."

"I'm sure I shall."

The woman murmured, "The stew."

"Yes," her husband said. "There's a pot of stew on the stove, so you won't starve."

"Thank you," Andrew said. "For everything. You have things nicely organised. I appreciate that."

"Well, Mr. Bailey, we appreciate your willingness to help us with this—um—problem."

"It's my job," Andrew said, and, because he knew the topic was delicate, changed it. Shrewdly, he started to talk of his work with retarded children. It had effect. The woman began to come back from her retreat. She looked at him occasionally and was beginning to ask questions by the time her husband said:

"Listen. We better start moving. Haig Wilson doesn't like to be kept waiting."

Rising, Andrew said, "I know that name—Haig Wilson."

"He's a reporter with the Toronto *Echo*."

"Of course." He turned to the woman. "Good night, Mrs. Scott. I'll see you tomorrow. Two colleagues will be here as well, if you can stand the crowd."

Her smile came close to being warm, real. "I'll try, Mr. Bailey. Good night."

Outside, Andrew got in his own car and followed Harry Scott's Cadillac when it came out of the carport. They went around the houses and along a dirt track. As with the approach, there was a belt of trees to pass through.

The sky had deepened to full night now. Andrew's headlights whitened a cluster of clapboard buildings, the most prominent a high hip-roof barn. Standing about were ancient pieces of equipment. One was a tractor like a primitive tank.

The cars went to the cluster's centre. Andrew was pleased with the large frame house. It had all the fuss and frills of its time, including false turrets and ornate eaves and fretwork around the front porch. Lights were on inside.

Getting out of his car, overnight bag in hand, Andrew said, "This looks more like a farm."

"Non-operational, to use one of Jack's terms," Harry Scott said. "But some of the buildings come in useful for storage. Nowadays, the farm centre's a mile from here. Very modern. Looks like a factory."

"Sounds as if you don't approve."

"I'm a romantic, Mr. Bailey. The kind that starves to death in garrets."

They went in the house—by the back door. There was warmth and a smell of food. After giving his guest a quick tour, Harry Scott left. Andrew had a more leisurely look around.

A conservationist would have been appalled at the changes and additions, as well as the mingling of modern furniture with the old. Andrew didn't care, but he did decide to make the kitchen his base, liking its unspoilt look and the rocking chairs.

On his way back from leaving his bag in the bedroom prepared for him, Andrew paused by the foot of the stairs. On the wall there hung a portrait in oils, which the host had indicated in passing with:

"Moina herself. Painted after her death from a photograph. The old girl would have been outraged at such a folly."

"Do you remember her yourself, Mr. Scott?"

"Only as someone I was supposed to be in awe of. And was."

The portrait showed a face that was still handsome in spite of the marks of age; a sombre, compelling face, with a good resemblance to that of the grandchild, Elaine. An enhancing feature, removing some of the severity, was the silver hair that fell in gentle waves.

"I wonder," Andrew said. He went on, and set about making himself at home.

An hour later, after a plate of stew, he was reading the first writings produced by Mrs. Scott, both in the original and in transcript. They were similar in style and matter to the one he had read at headquarters—rambling, disjointed talk of things and nature.

Andrew found that, from frequent checks of the handwritten versions with the typed, he was beginning to get an understanding of the former, could decipher many words and sentences. That was going to be useful.

From outside came the sound of a car stopping. Andrew got up and opened the door. Coming up onto the stoop was an attractive girl of about twenty. She was slight, thin-faced, and had brown hair styled in an urchin cut.

"Hello, Mr. Bailey," she said, voice and manner pert. "I'm Rennie Bates. The original Miss Efficiency."

Andrew grinned. "Which includes working after hours?"

"Sure—for time and a half."

Andrew brought her inside and sat with her at the kitchen table. "Can I offer you a coffee?"

"Thanks, no. Can't stay. Heavy date. But I will smoke a cig with you—if you have the vice."

"In spades, Miss Bates."

"Oh, call me Rennie, for heaven's sake. The other, it makes me feel like an old maid."

"Which, I'm sure, will never come to pass."

The girl took a cigarette, lit it from the proffered match, and asked, "Are all ghost hunters as smooth as you, Mr. Bailey?"

"Andrew. Yes. We get special training."

The light banter continued. Her animation could be

forced, Andrew thought, as if she were determined to be bright, or she might be covering another emotion, either for his sake or her own.

Rennie drew small-folded papers from her pocket. "Here's the latest instalment in the stirring saga."

Andrew asked, "Is that how you see this, as something not to be taken seriously?"

"Oh no. No way. I get gooseflesh just thinking about it. It's the most fabulous thing I've heard of in years. I hope it turns out to be real."

"What else could it be?"

"God knows," the secretary said. "That's your department. You tell me."

Andrew gave his standard, mysterious smile. He said, "The Scotts give the impression of being nice, average sort of people. Is that how you see them?"

Rennie Bates stubbed her cigarette. "Sure, just like you say. They're well liked in these parts, if that's what you're really asking. The Scotts have no side."

"Good."

"They're not at their best, of course, on account of the sadness. But that's easing. Except with Jack. He's still down there."

Andrew shook his head. "I'm not with you."

"Cissy Scott. Jack's wife. She died a year ago."

"I didn't know that."

"She was the sparkiest thing in the county," the girl said, getting up. "Jack Scott's only half there."

"It takes time."

A minute later, Rennie Bates gone, Andrew was unfolding the papers.

Ann prowled around the apartment, making a pretence at tidying. She was impatient and frustrated. Here she was city- and office-bound when by rights she should have been at the scene of the action. But Ann told herself: Calm, calm.

Already, while washing dishes after dinner, she had broken two plates, her imagination so busy conjuring up all the wonderful occult things that could be happening at the O'Neal place.

Ann winced as she trod on a pencil. She was in her bare feet so as not to disturb her parents, who had retired. For the same reason she had piled cushions on the telephone.

Now, when the expected call came at last, she hardly heard the ringing. She pounced, flung cushions aside, and grabbed up the receiver. She said, "You're late."

"You knew it was me, of course," Andrew said.

"Naturally."

"I'm late because I've been hobnobbing with this cute little secretary called Rennie Bates."

"There's another reason for me to loathe you to pieces."

"I believe I know the first."

"You should. It's you being on the spot instead of me."

"That's the way it has to be, sweet."

"Don't worry, I can take it and smile," Ann said. "You ought to see this smile."

"Okay now. Let me fill you in on my day."

Ann heard him out. She was annoyed and pleased that nothing had happened. She was able to say, "I missed you."

"Same here."

"And the old house sounds divine. Are you getting any signs or vibrations?"

"No, but that reminds me," Andrew said. "Please ask John to bring his whole bag of tricks, including the black box."

"That one? I hope you're sure about it."

"Certainly I am."

"Does Mrs. Scott know?"

"I haven't mentioned it yet. She or her husband might object if they knew beforehand. The smart thing is to ease 'em into it gently."

"Right," Ann said. "And you have today's automatic writing?"

"Yes. I've been over it twice. It's a good bit longer than the last one. You'll be seeing it yourself, but I can read you bits of it now."

"Does she mention names yet?"

"No. Listen. There's this bit.

"I don't know why the thunderheads make me nervous. They shouldn't. I like storms. Or anyway, I used to like storms. It's very exciting. The flash and cannon roar and the seething elements. Frightening, too. There's not a single thing you can do about it.'"

Ann said, "She's right there."

"And this from farther on.

"He looked at me today in such an odd sort of way. As if I had done something wrong. I can't imagine what it was for. I'm probably mistaken. I get such curious notions lately.'

"And this right at the end.

"I'm tired now from packaging all those clothes to send to the old folks' home. You wouldn't believe the work involved. But it's worth every minute and ache. Oh yes, and I've decided to send the things anonymously. Being thanked embarrasses me. I think maybe it's because I know that the receiver nearly always dislikes the Lady Bountiful. Therefore, of course, it isn't

embarrassment at all. It's self-protection. Spare me thy scorn.'"

Andrew said, "I wonder if you get what I seem to get from those pieces, Ann."

"What, for instance?"

"Well, there's an essence that wasn't in the earlier scripts. But it's been growing stronger in the later ones."

"Yes, but what?"

"It's a downbeat quality. A grimness, if you like. A sense of foreboding. There's less optimism."

"Yes," Ann said slowly. "I do get that. And the last one ended with a mention of shadows."

"That's it exactly. It's like a growing suspense."

"Any theories?"

"None at the moment," Andrew said. "Now tell me again about how you missed me."

When the call ended, Ann told herself she could relax, have a nightcap of rum and hot milk, go to bed. She nodded at the common sense of that and started again to prowl around the apartment.

Andrew jerked upright from the pillow. Immediately he was wide awake. He sat staring into the total darkness and wondered where he was. That came to him: in bed in the old O'Neal home.

Bringing his hand close to his face, he saw by the luminous dial of his watch that it was almost midnight. Now he queried what it could have been that had ripped him from sleep.

That was also answered, for he heard a sound. It was like a piece of furniture being moved along the floor. The source could have been from anywhere in the old house.

And it could be perfectly natural, Andrew assured himself. The creak and snap of shifting wood fibres you always got in frame buildings when there were temperature changes.

So why didn't he lie down and go back to sleep? Why was he still sitting, listening? Why was he nervous?

Because of the genes, Andrew thought. They passed on a piece of cave-man information: Be afraid of the dark. It is your enemy. It helps the predator get close.

The noise came again.

Andrew pushed back the covers. He slid down off the high old-fashioned bed. With both hands out, leading the way, he edged blindly across the room. Sweat tickled his armpits.

He found the wall, the door, the light switch. At a touch of his fingers the blackness vanished. The glow from the table lamps was pink and pleasant.

It enabled Andrew to smile at his foolishness at troubling to get out of bed. Was he going to lose sleep over a shutter swinging in the wind, a warped floor board, a fault in the heating?

Anywhere else, the answer would have been no. Here was different. This was part of his job.

Andrew went to the bed and put on his robe and slippers. Back at the door, he switched off the light. He found his tension returning in the darkness. But he stood on there, his head close to the wood. He could hear nothing. And there was no wind.

The silence ended. From downstairs had come a repeat of the noise, though now it was louder and with an air of finality, as if a job had been completed and all was ready.

Softly, Andrew turned the handle. He began to open the door. He stopped at once when the hinges wailed. There was no form of response to the sound from elsewhere in the house.

Recalling an old trick that had been told him by a burglar, Andrew did the reverse of the instinctive. Rather than gentling the door he jerked it open fast. There was no wail.

He had expected to find a matching darkness out in the passage. Instead, there was a dim yellow gleam. It came from the left, toward the stairs. All was silent in the house.

Treading quietly, Andrew left the room. His jaw was firm, his eyes steady. He knew he had switched off all the lights before coming upstairs.

He also knew that one of the Scotts, who had every right, could have come in the house to get something, or for one of a dozen other reasons.

Because of that, Andrew realised that the sensible thing would be to call out, ask who was there. But in his profession it wasn't always the sensible thing that worked.

Still moving slowly, he was nearing the stairhead. The light from below had gained only minimally in strength. That gave him a possible solution. He could have left the icebox door open forgetfully: its low light was permeating the ground floor, its frozen goods were shifting noisily as they warmed.

Andrew didn't believe it for a moment. And he assured himself that he wasn't nervous, merely alert.

He came to the head of the stairs. He stopped. Most of the parlour below was in view. The light was strong enough for him to see that everything looked the same as before.

The light's source was plain. It was from beyond an open doorway, one that Andrew recalled as belonging to a sewing room.

There was still no sound.

Andrew started down the stairs. He wondered if it were stupid of him to be doing this unarmed. There could be a burglar in the house.

He didn't believe that either.

The light, Andrew noted, seemed to be moving gently.

That is, the shadows it made were unsteady, flowing. He felt a prickling among the hairs on the back of his neck.

A primordial reaction, he thought. The animal in him was responding warily to the unknown.

He came to the bottom step. The woman gazed at him steadily, her eyes mysterious. He nodded at the painting and went on.

Quietly he moved across the parlour. He circled furniture, heading for the open doorway. Even before reaching it he saw, through there, the source of the light. It was an oil lamp.

Andrew went into the sewing room cautiously. It was deserted. He stepped to the centre table and leaned close to the lamp. It was old, with an ornate bowl half full of liquid and a tall glass funnel. The flame on the wick was undulating slightly.

After staring at the lamp for a moment, Andrew turned away. He left the room and checked the rest of the ground floor, every corner and closet, finishing in the kitchen. He had seen nothing else amiss—at least, not in his limited knowledge of the house.

When he switched on the kitchen light, however, he noticed that something seemed to be either missing or out of its former position. He looked around carefully while getting his cigarettes from the table and lighting up.

He saw what was wrong. The rocking chairs. There had been three. Now there were two.

Andrew made straight for the sewing room. The chair was there, its back turned, facing the tall writing desk in a corner, the desk in which the O'Neal papers were kept. Andrew went across to it.

The white figure made him start.

His breath jerked in. His heart left out two of its beats.

His nerves jangled. His muscles jammed as one fought another in trying to retreat.

Recovery was fast. Andrew saw the figure for what it was: a nightdress. The long white garment with a high, frilly neck lay in the rocking chair, its sleeves on the armrests. The impression was that the wearer had magically dissolved.

Andrew stepped back and picked up the cigarette he had dropped. He drew hungrily at the smoke. When he blew it out again in a long, lingering stream, it came from between smiling lips.

THREE

There were five people at the table having lunch, in addition to Ann: the Scott brothers, Elaine, Andrew, and John Bright, all spaced well apart around the large table in the Harry Scotts' dining room.

The talk, annoyingly for Ann, was on the mundane theme of how fast and vast Toronto was growing. Worse, no one disagreed with anyone else. It was a polite gathering.

Ann hid a yawn with her napkin. The day was turning out a bore, she thought, and she had been so excited on the drive out. She had even been indifferent to John's remarks on her driving.

Earlier, at headquarters, Ann had received a call from Andrew. After telling her that he wanted additional equipment, he had told of his midnight experience.

Trying to keep the envy out of her voice, Ann had said—stated—"A visitation."

"Let's not leap to any conclusions, Ann."

"Did you check the doors?"

"Naturally. And I went over the house again, searched it from top to bottom. The doors weren't bolted on the inside and the locks are the normal type. You see?"

"No."

"I mean that anyone with a key or felonious knowledge could have got in."

"A lot of trouble for some living person to go to, and for no real accomplishment."

Andrew had said, "Do ghosts move furniture and get old clothes out of cedar chests? Do they put in working order oil lamps that haven't been used for years?"

"You don't know that—about the lamp."

"Not for certain, but I found the shelf in a larder that it came from. There's a dustless circle beside four other lamps. And they are all without kerosene."

Ann had asked, "Are you going to tell the Scotts about what happened?"

"Haven't decided yet."

"Moina's chair, Moina's nightgown, Moina's writing desk. It sounds very good to me."

"Sounds to me," Andrew had said, "as if someone's giving me a message, and not one from the grave."

"You mean someone's trying to scare you off?"

"Could be."

"That's silly. I prefer the supranormal angle."

"Do ghosts smoke?"

"Andrew," Ann had complained, "I do wish you wouldn't use old-fashioned terms like that. Presence, entity, spirit. They sound much better, more adult."

"Yes, ma'am. But whatever, I found a cigarette butt on the back stoop."

Later, in the flurry of arrival, Ann had not had a chance to talk privately to Andrew. She wanted to urge him to reveal what he had seen last night. It could, she felt, have significance in relation to the phenomenon of automatic writing.

Now, for the second time, Ann caught Andrew's eye, trying to get her meaning across to him. He looked away as before. Ann wished the table were narrower, so she could reach him in the surest way, with a kick.

Yet she knew that it might not work. Andrew tended to get secretive in investigations, even with her. He became

miserly with whatever clues and information he came
across.

"That chop all right, Miss Goodwin?"

Ann turned quickly to the speaker, Jack Scott. "Fine,
thank you. Delicious. In fact I was just wondering why we
don't get meat like this in the city."

"Try changing your butcher. Find one who appreciates a
pretty face."

Which Ann considered charming while not being at all
charmed. She had not taken to this brisk man, any more
than she had warmed to his sister-in-law.

Ann looked at her hostess, who was pecking at her food as
languorously as she had all along—twice her husband had
said, gently, "You're not eating, dear." She had been the
same about the conversation: aloof, disinterested, dipping in
only for the occasional morsel.

She acted, Ann thought, as though she were double her
real age. She was like a movie queen who had drearily accepted the decline of both fame and beauty. But she was
also of the type, ennui-ridden, that is open to distant
influences. Her mind was like an empty house waiting to be
occupied.

"The house," Ann said abruptly. Everyone looked at her.
She fumbled, "Um—the old place where Moina O'Neal
lived. I'm dying to see it."

Harry Scott said, "It's a reasonably classic example of the
period, isn't it, Elaine?"

His wife gave a slight nod. "Yes."

Ann asked, "Has it been modernised? You know, has it
got electricity, lights, and everything?" She was avoiding
looking at Andrew but could nevertheless tell that he was
glaring at her.

Jack Scott launched into a detailed account of the problems of modernising old buildings, directing most of his talk to John Bright. Ann smiled sweetly at Andrew.

After Mrs. Maynard had brought in coffee and a cheese board, Harry Scott said, in an untidy attempt at businesslike heartiness:

"Well, Mr. Bailey, what's going to be the next step in your investigation?"

Andrew waved out a match from lighting a cigarette. "I'm hoping, of course, to be present at an entrancement. That's most important, obviously."

"It's bound to happen sooner or later."

"Meanwhile, after lunch, John and I would like to go over this house."

Elaine Scott looked up from her coffee. "Why?"

Andrew said, "I'd like to be able to put in my report that the place was checked thoroughly and that nothing of a suspicious nature was found."

Harry Scott turned from face to face. "Suspicious nature? I don't get that."

"I can't be explicit, but the house should be checked. With your permission, of course. I've no idea what we might find that could relate to the phenomena."

John Bright leaned forward. "We had a case once," he said, "where the occupier of the house kept having fainting spells whenever he went into a certain room. Physically he was in top condition, had been examined thoroughly more than once. The room, we found, had a gas leak."

Giving his head a slow, puzzled shake, Harry Scott said, "I still don't see . . ."

Neither did Ann. She wondered what Andrew's real reason was for a search of the house; and when was he going to bring up the subject of the black box?

Mrs. Scott became almost voluble, though still without

animation. "It's quite all right with me," she said. "I have to go into town."

Jack Scott said, "The angle you people are working on, then, is that this is not supernatural."

"I'm not," Ann said forcefully. "I'm prepared to believe that it's a true case of automatic writing. Another Patience Worth, if that name means anything."

Elaine Scott was looking at her. "It rings a tiny bell," she said.

Ann outlined the story. The Scott brothers listened keenly, Elaine with her usual passive expression.

Andrew said, "There are dozens of such cases on record that have never been disproved."

"And hundreds that have," John Bright capped.

Jack Scott turned to him. "Would you care to give us your view of this, Mr. Bright?"

The lab man shrugged, smiling. "It could have some natural cause—a condition within Mrs. Scott herself. It could have an accidental cause—like that gas thing."

"I see."

John Bright added, "It could also be phony."

Harry Scott sat straighter. "Phony?"

Andrew said a hurried, diplomatic "What John's trying to say is that the writing could be produced consciously, for some personal reason."

Jack Scott: "Name one."

"One?" John Bright said. "Okay. How about money? These cases always attract a great deal of attention. The media have a ball. A book written by one of the people involved would be a sure-fire best seller, for instance. The Patience Worth affair must've earned thousands."

Ann, embarrassed, was trying to shrink into her chair. The atmosphere had dropped by several degrees. However, Mrs. Scott's voice was unchanged when she said:

"We are not, Mr. Bright, short of money."

Her husband cleared his throat and looked pointedly at his watch. Lunch was over.

As they all rose, Ann said, "I wonder if I might come to town with you, Mrs. Scott? I'd love to see the district."

The hostess returned an automatic "Be glad of your company." She excused herself to go and get ready.

Ann had a chance to talk privately to Andrew when, in the kitchen, he was helping her on with her coat. He said, "I spent an hour with Elaine this morning, talking the situation over. I didn't get very far. She's locked away inside."

"It certainly looks that way. Which is encouraging. My hopes are high."

"See if you can get more friendly with her, Ann. You've made a good start. She might unbend to you."

Ann said, "I'll do my damnedest."

"And no mention of oil lamps, rocking chairs, or nightgowns. That's my department."

"Yes, sir."

Harry Scott appeared beside them. He said, his tone low and confidential, "There could be another trance today. I know the warning signs. It looks good."

"As your wife had one yesterday," Andrew said, "that would mean they're getting more frequent."

"Yes. Is it a bad omen?"

"That I can't tell. The reverse, I should think."

"I agree," Ann said. "The reverse."

The host shook his head. "God, I'll be glad when this is all over." He turned with a smile as his wife came into the kitchen.

Outside with Elaine Scott, Ann pointed to her Volkswagen. "Do you mind if we use my car? The battery's low and I need to juice it up a bit."

Mrs. Scott shook her head, and Ann smiled. She wanted to give the woman every opportunity to go into a trance.

When the Scott brothers had driven off in a pickup, Andrew went back to the kitchen. Mrs. Maynard looked around from stacking plates in the dishwasher. She said:

"I know, I know. I'll be gone in a minute."

"I hate to send you out in the cold, ma'am."

"Don't fret on my account, young man. I'll do the tidy-up next door that I usually do."

Andrew waited a moment before saying, "By the way, that dessert you served us was wonderful. Dare I ask you for the recipe?"

The housekeeper's manner became less fussed. "Surely. It's nothing special. I'll write it out for you when I have a spare second to myself."

"I'd be grateful," Andrew said, backing off.

He returned to the living room where John Bright, lounging on a couch, said, "I have several questions, Chief."

Andrew went to stand with his back to the imitation fire. "I know. And number one is why did I want to get that recipe."

"More or less. I was going to ask since when have you been interested in cooking. You can hardly boil an egg."

"True. What I'm after is a sample of Mrs. Maynard's writing. Also of the others'."

"Well, well."

"We might be able to get some now, come to think of it. Then we'd have a real reason for having the house to ourselves."

"There goes one of my questions. What, in fact, are we here for?"

"Primarily," Andrew said, "it was to see if anyone objected, or came back to run interference, or put certain areas off limits. Two have been cleared. The interference, that remains to be seen. I doubt it."

"So do I. There's no gadgetry to be discovered in a case like this. And I didn't get the impression that anyone was doing a fast hiding job before leaving the house."

"A minor reason was to pick up latent prints to match with what we may find at the old place."

"All right," the lab man said. "Now tell me why you want writing samples."

Andrew teetered on his toes. "What no one seems to have realised, including me up till a short while ago, is that these scripts could have been produced by someone other than Mrs. Scott. If she's in a genuine non-conscious state, she wouldn't know. And it's already been established that the writing bears little resemblance to her normal hand."

"True," John Bright said thoughtfully. "All you'd need to do is put the pages on her knee and tell her she did it."

"It's an angle. We have to consider everything. Now let's poke about."

"I'll get my case from the hall."

"And, John," Andrew said, "remind me to have a chat with you sometime about tact."

The technician laughed.

They were in the house an hour. Nobody came. John Bright found and photographed useful prints on the dishwasher, Harry Scott's hairbrush and Elaine Scott's vanity table. He was diligent about cleaning up the blackpowder evidence.

He used the same camera to take pictures of the Scotts' handwriting, taking more than one example: letters, an appointment calendar, the stub of a checkbook, the backs of snapshots.

These last were in an album found by Andrew. He went through it, and then through others from the same cupboard. Clothing and film quality changed as the albums covered older ground. There were many photographs of the younger Moina O'Neal, vital-looking, her long black hair hanging free and her eyes bright. In some poses she was with her second husband, a rangy, gaunt man with a drooping moustache.

After Andrew had gone carefully through a bathroom medicine chest, the work was over. They went outside. About to drive off, Andrew paused, seeing a car approaching. He noted, as it came onto the forecourt, that the driver was a man whose face was familiar.

Andrew opened the door. "Slide over, John. You go on and get to work. The house is unlocked."

The other car had stopped. Andrew walked over to it as the lab technician drove away. The newcomer got out. He was blond and tanned, and handsome enough to be an actor.

"You must be Andrew Bailey," he said, offering his hand. "The ghost hunter."

"And you're Haig Wilson. I've seen your picture at the head of your column."

"You're a sports fan?"

Managing to hide a wince at the strength of the man's grip, Andrew said, "I sure am. But some events I'd rather read about than see."

"You just made yourself a friend for life."

After a minute of casual talk, Haig Wilson said, "Jack around, d'you know?"

Andrew explained the situation, finishing with, "I don't know when they'll be back."

"I'll find him. The thing is, I have a couple of tickets for the wrestling tonight in Toronto. Cheer old Jack up a bit."

"He's feeling the loss of his wife strongly, it seems."

"It's a rotten business," Haig Wilson said, "murder."

Andrew got out his cigarettes, offered them, had the offer declined, lit one for himself. Blowing out smoke, he said, "Murder?"

The sports writer raised his eyebrows. "You didn't know how Cissy Scott died?"

"Only that she had."

"Well, come to think of it, I don't suppose there was any reason for anyone to tell you. And you wouldn't remember it from the papers. It was no headliner."

"Maybe you'd better tell me about it, if you don't mind."

"Almost a year ago," Haig Wilson said. "It happened about a mile from here. Elaine and Cissy were doing their Halloween thing of visiting tenants. It was dark. They parked the car in a clump of trees on the edge of the road. Elaine got out and went to the nearby house. That's when the guy killed Cissy."

"Who was he?" Andrew asked. "What happened?"

"The guy, they caught him within a week. A nut. A mentally deficient farm boy from this area. He's in an institution, unfit to plead to the charge. He'd made other attacks on women before that night."

"He attacked Jack's wife? Randomly?"

"That's it, the theory."

Andrew asked, "She hadn't known him before that night?"

"Not from Adam," the reporter said. "He's just a kid, around twenty, if that."

"What did he kill her with?"

"The gun. Cissy was armed. Because of these attacks that had happened—'molestations' is a better word—naturally the girls had a gun in the car. But apparently the guy got it away from Cissy, or it went off while he was trying to do that. Anyway, she was shot and killed."

Andrew shook his head. "Terrible. I know how Jack must

feel. It's worse somehow than a natural death. It can't have been easy for Elaine, either."

"Right. Her being there and all, apart from the loss. They were pretty close."

"And," Andrew said, "there'd be additional emotional stress afterwards. Elaine would be sharing grief with relief. It could've been her instead of Cissy. It would be unnatural if she didn't count herself lucky."

"Right," Haig Wilson said. "I'd be the same."

"It would've been better if Cissy Scott hadn't pulled the gun, maybe. How about the previous attacks by this man?"

"Nothing much. The women were more frightened than hurt. That's why the Scott girls decided not to cancel the outing, and why it was fixed that the first shell in the revolver was a blank."

"Scare anyone off, sure, and no harm done."

Haig Wilson said, "The trauma of it all could have been building up quietly in Elaine. Could be it's that that's started this so-called automatic writing."

"You think there's nothing to it?"

"Right. I think it's a symptom. That girl needs help, and the sooner the better."

Andrew dropped his cigarette and slowly swivelled it out underfoot. He said, "I'm not so sure about that. I could be wrong, I have been before, but I feel there's a lot of reserve strength in that woman."

The reporter said, "Let's hope time proves you right."

Declining a ride from Haig Wilson, Andrew set out to walk to the old house. He went through a doorway in the carport's rear wall and across a lawn. Nearing the trees, he glanced back. Watching him from a window in Jack's house was plump and comfortable Mrs. Maynard. He waved. She nodded and turned away.

At the old place, Andrew found that John Bright had finished dusting for fingerprints in the sewing room. Aiming his camera, he asked, "Did you touch any of these things?"

"The chair, no. The lamp, only that little gizmo that winds the wick up or down."

"That's fine. There's some nice stuff here, on both articles. Three or four sets."

Andrew indicated the nightdress. "How about that?"

The lab technician looked at him scornfully. "Soft material? Really, Chief. Now something that's been starched, that's a different story."

He went on snapping pictures. When the last had been taken, he said, "As soon as I've cleaned up here, these things can be put back."

Andrew shook his head deliberately. "No way. They stay exactly where they are."

The sewing-room work completed, John Bright set about fixing up a trip line across the bottom of the doorway between kitchen and parlour. It would activate a hidden camera.

"I very much doubt if it'll be needed," Andrew said. "If my visitor last night was of flesh and blood, he'd be foolish to come back. I've been tipped off."

"Never reckon on people being sensible," John said. "You taught me that yourself."

"Which is why I'm having you do this."

John Bright straightened from his squat, having set the line aside. "Put it back before you go to bed. It's a fine thread that'll break on contact. The visitor won't feel a thing."

He was fixing the hair-trigger camera behind a curtain when Ann arrived. She looked agitated.

"Hi," Andrew said. "What's biting you?"

Ann took off her coat and flung it onto a chair. "I hate like hell to leave that woman. She could go into a trance at any time. You heard what her husband said. I'll kick myself around the block if I miss it."

Andrew shrugged. "Can't very well trail her about indefinitely."

"More's the pity. But there must be something we can do." Ann came to him quickly. "Listen. Here's what's just occurred to me. Why don't we invite the Scotts here for supper? Sort of return engagement while I'm still on the scene."

"That, my sweet, is a great idea."

"I could nip back to the village and buy some steaks."

"Call the house and see."

Ann went to the telephone. Andrew watched her with satisfaction and pride while she made the call, and laughed when she dropped the receiver into its cradle with a hoot of triumph.

Andrew began to tell Ann how they had got on at the Scott house. When he had finished, she said, "So it was bluff."

"Mainly. But what about you and Elaine? Did she thaw any?"

Ann flapped her arms against her sides. "She's a hard one to crack. Speaks when she's spoken to, like a polite child. It was all 'Yes, Miss Goodwin,' and 'No, Miss Goodwin.' Pretty exhausting, and for nothing."

"Have you formed an opinion of her?"

"Not really. You can't when a person's only partly there— and what is there is wound up tight. But I'll tell you one thing. Elaine Scott is either suffering from depression or is badly frightened."

Getting down from a chair, John Bright said, "Or is a neat actress."

"No, John. It's no act."

"It's been made clear," Andrew said, "that she's unhappy

about these trances. That sort of thing can be very scary. Imagine it happening to you."

Gravely, Ann said, "I'd be overjoyed."

Andrew sidestepped to "So the outing was uneventful."

"Except for meeting your young secretary, yes. She asked after your health. Terribly sweet of her."

John Bright made a sound like a cat and Andrew said, "You met her where?"

"Library. We went there, a drugstore for coffee, and a supermarket. It's a cute little town."

"In the drugstore," Andrew asked, "did Elaine go to the prescription counter?"

"No, Andrew. I was alert to every move, believe me. I never left her side."

"Okay. Good girl."

Ann said, "Now, before I go shopping, let me look around this divine old house."

Andrew held up his hand. "Let me tell you first what I heard from our star reporter Haig Wilson."

"Murder," Jack Scott said. "The thing that always happens to other people, never your own."

"How awful," Ann murmured, and felt the inadequacy of her words. She regretted her initial dislike of the man. Naturally he had little in the way of warmth to communicate—he had none for himself.

Andrew said, "Perhaps I shouldn't have brought it up. Sorry. It was thoughtless of me."

"No, that's all right," Jack Scott said. "And as you pointed out, it might have a bearing on this affair."

"It's an outside possibility."

They were in the old-fashioned kitchen, standing around the table, the men holding glasses, Ann chopping vegetables. As Jack Scott was unable to make supper, having a date to go to the wrestling matches in the city with Haig Wilson, he had stopped in before the others to have a drink.

There was silence. It was punctuated by Ann's chopping and the sounds from the parlour of John Bright trying to get a fire going in the hearth.

"The tradition was started by Moina O'Neal," Jack Scott said, as if he had been prompted by Ann's wish to know more. "On Halloween she'd dress as a witch and go calling on the farm workers. She had food for the adults, gifts for the kids. Elaine's father let it lapse, but she started the thing going again. In recent years, she and Cissy did it together. They had a ball, dressing up and everything."

"Sounds gorgeous," Ann said. "And what a wonderful idea. Treats with no tricks."

"That night they were dressed as white witches, cone hats and all the trimmings. They borrowed the costumes from the barn theatre, the local amateur group. Cissy was its leading light. She was good, too. Everyone said so."

While Ann and Andrew made appropriate murmurs, Scott brought out a billfold. He opened it, saying, "And beautiful enough to be in movies."

After Andrew had looked at the photograph he held the billfold for Ann to see. The coloured studio portrait showed an attractive, smiling woman with a pale complexion and dark curly hair. Again, Ann and Andrew made the right comments.

Jack Scott put his billfold away carefully. He said, "It happened not a mile from here. If I'd been outdoors I would've heard the shooting. I was in old Jim Webber's, playing cards."

Andrew said, "It was probably a good thing you didn't hear it. Not a pleasant memory to have. Also, you wouldn't have been able to do anything."

"Except maybe get there in time to chase the guy," Jack

Scott said. "Or see my . . ." He stopped, drew a breath, turned away.

There was another silence. Ann looked imploringly at Andrew: Talk about something else.

"Er—that man you mentioned," Andrew said. "Webber, was it? Is he a real old-timer in these parts?"

Jack Scott took a drink before turning. His face was void of expression. He said, "Old Jim's been here forever. Retired now. We rent him what we call the gatehouse."

"Would that be the place where your service lane meets the public road?"

"That's it. He raises a few vegetables out back."

"I'd like to talk to him," Andrew said. "If he goes back to Moina O'Neal's day."

As Jack Scott nodded, there came the sound from outside of car doors slamming. Ann said, "Damn. I knew I wouldn't be ready in time."

She felt better a few minutes later when, greetings over, Andrew took the three guests away, saying he wanted them to explain a picture in the sewing room.

Immediately after they had left, John Bright slipped into the kitchen. He hissed, "Which is Jack's glass?" When Ann pointed it out, he picked it up with a pair of tweezers and carried it off.

Next, Ann heard sounds of exclamation. Putting down the knife, she went into the parlour, stopping where she had a clear view into the sewing room. The visitors and Andrew were standing near the writing desk.

"How did that nightdress get here?" Elaine Scott asked, using a tone with a shade more vigor than formerly.

Her husband said, "And that lamp. It was in the pantry last time I saw it." He bent closer. "There's fuel in it, too."

"The nightdress is one of Granny's. It should be in a chest in her room. I keep all her things there."

In an amused voice her brother-in-law asked, "What's it all about, Mr. Bailey? Does this help in some way?"

Andrew put out his hands. "Wait a minute. This is how I found these things. Isn't the lamp always here? I did wonder about the nightgown."

"And the rocking chair," Harry Scott said. "That's from the kitchen. I saw it there last night."

Andrew said, "Everything's just as I found it this morning when I came down. What could it mean?"

After a pause, during which the Scotts exchanged looks, Harry said, his tone cool, "I think you must know the answer, Mr. Bailey. Possibly this is part of your regular routine in these cases, like the house search this afternoon. Though I fail to see the motive."

His brother's voice was still amused as he asked, "Trying to raise the old girl's spirit, Mr. Bailey?"

Andrew protested. He was still doing that—though the others were sounding disinterested—when Ann retreated to the kitchen. She told herself that this was not likely to be a successful dinner party.

She was right. After Jack Scott left, Andrew served drinks to the remaining guests and did his best to make conversation. At one point, he and John Bright were the only ones talking. Ann called them all into the kitchen, where she served the meal. The steaks, as luck would have it, were tough. The guests ate hardly anything. Again, talk limped. The longest exchange was:

Andrew: "Whatever became of Moina O'Neal's second husband, by the way?"

Harry Scott: "She divorced him."

Andrew: "Yes, I know. Did he stay on around here?"

Harry Scott: "No, he went out to British Columbia, and then into the States."

Andrew: "I guess he'll be dead by now."

Harry Scott: "Donkey's years ago. In San Francisco."

Ann kept thinking that the party had to get better because it couldn't get worse. But she was wrong. After she had served her speciality of shredded cheese in yogurt, Andrew brought up the question of the black box.

Elaine Scott said, "I beg your pardon?"

"A lie-detector test," Andrew repeated. He spoke casually, as if this were an everyday matter. "John brought the equipment along with him."

Harry Scott asked, "You mean you actually want my wife to subject herself to a test to see if she's lying?"

Andrew put on an expression of bewilderment, which Ann considered badly done. "But it's standard procedure in every case we handle. It didn't occur to me that there might be an objection. If, that is, you do object."

"That's not the issue," Elaine Scott said stiffly. "Do you believe that I'm lying?"

Ann took a turn, offering with a smile, "Mr. Bailey has a completely open mind, Mrs. Scott. He needs this test to clear away any doubt in connection with deception."

"And any possible deception," Andrew said, "need not necessarily be to your knowledge. A test could, in fact, clear up this whole matter at once, and to everyone's satisfaction."

Except mine, Ann thought. She tensed when John Bright cleared his throat; but all he said was a helpful "The test's quite simple, ma'am. Doesn't hurt a bit."

Elaine Scott frowned. "I hate gadgets."

"I can have it over with inside half an hour."

Andrew said, "You are, of course, perfectly at liberty to decline to take the test."

Harry Scott looked at his wife. "It's up to you, dear."

She sighed and said tiredly, "Oh, I don't suppose it matters. Yes, I'll take it. But not tonight."

John nodded at Andrew. "That's okay, Chief. I can come back in the morning."

They left it there, to Ann's relief, and the dinner went on its way more feebly than ever. It was like a funeral meal when the heirs are disappointed.

Ann served coffee in the parlour. Elaine Scott, sitting in a corner of the couch, stared into the fire. Her husband assisted in a mainly one-sided conversation with Andrew on Canadian poets. Ann felt guilty about glancing at her watch, until she noticed that others seemed to be making the act into a habit.

Harry Scott palmed back a yawn. He got up and said, "Well, I guess it's time we were running along."

With the exception of Mrs. Scott, everyone rose. Andrew asked, "Would ten o'clock in the morning be all right for us to come and run the test?"

"Ten it is," Harry Scott said. "We'll be waiting." He went to the couch, bent over and took Elaine by the wrists. He began to straighten. "Let's go, honey."

Ann was startled by what happened next. She winced and took a step back.

Elaine Scott suddenly turned animated. Her body tensed and her eyes flashed. She ripped free of her husband's clasp and snapped, "Don't do that!"

He stammered, "Well—I—sorry—" He blinked, bemused.

The atmosphere changed from boredom to embarrassment. While Elaine Scott subsided, hunching with arms forward and head down, a sulking position, the others all started talking at once.

Harry Scott, flushed, said it had been a fine evening, just fine. Ann apologised again for the steak. John Bright insisted that he didn't mind at all coming back out tomorrow. Andrew said how much he liked the old house.

The minor hubbub, slowing in pace, lasted until the lab man hissed, "Look at that."

It was Elaine. Her position had changed to a sag. Her hands were lying in her lap. Her eyelids were lowered.

Harry Scott whispered, "That's it. She's in a trance."

Andrew stepped swiftly to the couch and knelt down. He looked into the woman's face, then placed his fingers on the side of her neck. After a moment he said:

"Pulse slower than normal."

John Bright, moving close with the others, asked, "What about temperature?"

"Seems okay. Could we get an accurate reading without using mouth or armpit?"

"Not really. If she feels normal, that'll do."

"Get a camera."

"Yes, Chief."

"No," Ann said urgently. "Writing material first. Look." She pointed.

Elaine Scott's right hand, the thumb and forefinger pincered, was making small, circular motions on her thigh.

John Bright left. He was back almost at once with a pad of note paper and a pen, which he eased gently into the woman's hand, putting the pad into position on her lap.

Elaine Scott immediately began to write.

Ann sank happily into a chair.

An hour later the old house was quiet. Andrew sat alone in the kitchen. After the Scotts had gone, the OSPR team had discussed the evening at length. Andrew was particularly interested in the others' opinion of the trance. Genuine, Ann had stated firmly. John Bright hadn't been sure, and his doubt was intriguing to Andrew.

The script, after being photographed by John, who had also taken scores of shots of the entranced woman, had been taken away by the Scotts, to be turned over to Rennie Bates for transcription.

After Andrew had kissed Ann good night at the Volkswagen, she had said smugly, "Well, that knocks one theory on the head: that someone else was doing the writing. 'Night, sweet."

Andrew got up and began to pace. He was stimulated, restless. He went through the parlour into the sewing room, which had been returned to its original state. Before sitting at the desk and pulling down its flap, he thought of the Scotts' reaction to seeing what the midnight visitor had arranged.

That reaction had been a disappointment, in so far as it was what would be expected from innocent parties. The only conclusion Andrew had reached was that the three were seeing the things here for the first time or were well in control of themselves.

Andrew began to dip into Moina O'Neal's papers. This he gave up after ten minutes. He was too restless for quiet study; he needed to be active. Also, he had the feeling that something was happening, or should be happening.

He went to get his topcoat.

Before leaving the house, on an afterthought, Andrew put the trip line into place across the bottom of the kitchen-parlour door.

Outside, he set off walking. The night was clear, starry, with enough light to see the way. There was a snap of frost in the air, like tension.

Andrew soon reached the twin houses. Jack Scott's was in darkness. The other had lights in several windows, and, as Andrew skirted it, he heard the hollow tones of a television set.

He went around the forecourt on top of its edging wall, arms out for balance, and then along the lane. The tarmac surfacing, an expensive piece of work, reminded Andrew of what Mrs. Scott had said: the O'Neal farm was not short of money. That was another theory weakened, if not destroyed.

A light showed ahead. It was on the side of the small frame house by the gateway. A minute later Andrew was there, knocking on the door.

Following a short wait, a cracked voice called, "Who'n the hell's that?"

Andrew said, "My name's Bailey. I'm a guest of the Scotts."

The door opened. In the frame stood a painfully thin man of under average height. He had an eagle face with bald pate to match. The dark sweater that reached his knees hung on him like a bell tent that had collapsed around its pole.

"Sure," Jim Webber said, rubbing one eye with a fist. "You're the spook catcher. I heard all about you."

"And I've heard about you, sir."

"Don't call me sir, son. Makes me feel old. Which I ain't. Just plain Jim'll do."

"I'll watch that, Jim," Andrew said. "I hope I didn't call too late."

"Hell, no, I'm up half the night," the old man said. "I was a-settin' there showing myself card tricks."

"I can never do those things."

"Tell the God Almighty's truth, I'm not so hot at it either. But it only needs practice. And I got years to do that." He cocked his head birdlike. "Play cribbage?"

"As if I'd invented it."

"Come in," Jim Webber said shortly. Leading the way inside, he went on, "And the inventor was a poet called Lowell, him as wrote that iron bars don't make a prison."

Stone walls do not a prison make,/Nor iron bars a cage,

Andrew quoted to himself, adding: Richard Lovelace. But he said, "Well, that's interesting." He wasn't about to sour a useful source of information.

The living room was soap-smelling clean and rigidly tidy. The main seating ensemble was a card table sided by two high-backed armchairs. Sitting there, Andrew and Jim Webber were soon intent on their game of cribbage. Andrew waited awhile before saying:

"I understand you're no newcomer to the area, Jim."

"Born here, son," the old man mumbled, peering at his cards. "Left in ma teens, came home for a stretch, went off again to see a bit more of the world, then came back to settle for good. I been around, you might say."

"You might indeed. More than I have."

Jim Webber became expansive on the subject of travel to broaden the mind. Andrew, liking the man, allowed him his brag for that reason as much as to suit his purpose.

The game went on, both with the cards and in question and answer.

Sure, Jim liked the Scotts, fine folk that wasn't too snooty. Elaine's dad, he was a bit wishy-washy. Moina O'Neal was more down to earth. Sharp as a tack, too. Brain as good as any man's. The husband? Man by the name of Alex Carnov. A Rushing. Not a bad fella. But they didn't hit it off. Say, that Moina couldn't've been an angel to live with. Used to being the boss, see. Other folk who was here in Moina's day? Sure, lots of 'em. Lemme see now.

Andrew made a mental note of the names. He said, "I envy you your good memory, Jim. Mine's like a sieve."

"Eat more fish," the old man said. He tapped a yawn with his cards. "Fish is good for the memory."

Andrew moved his peg on the board. "Since you've heard of me, you must know the reason I'm here."

"No secret about that, far as I know."

"Good," Andrew said. "So tell me, what d'you think about this automatic writing?"

Jim Webber made a sound that was midway between a snort and a laugh. "Son, I think the little lady needs a nice long sea voyage."

Andrew smiled. "Never know, you could be right." He went back to asking about Moina O'Neal and her time.

Andrew set off walking from what the Scotts called the gatehouse. He was tired but contented. The day, he mused, had been interesting and lucrative. Some of the case's bits and pieces were beginning to stick together, and others seemed to have inclinations toward one another.

Andrew likened the bits of evidence to a mob of children playing in a schoolyard. The investigation's end would be when he tossed in the right piece of candy. The strong would rush forward and jam together.

Turning up his topcoat collar, Andrew headed for the belt of trees that hid the twin houses. His shoes rang loudly on the tarmac, the sound like that from a dawdling horse. Every time he breathed out he was in a brief mist.

The explosion shocked him.

He stopped and teetered backward. His hands flew from his pockets to a protective position high in front. He gave a noisy gasp.

The silence following the explosion was awesome. There was not a sound to be heard. Andrew began to wonder if he had imagined the violent crash from beyond the trees.

From the other way, behind him, came another, smaller noise: the slam of a door. Andrew glanced back. Jim Webber was coming, struggling into an overcoat. The explosion had not been imaginary.

Andrew started to run.

Now the night was full of sounds. Andrew's footsteps and

those of the man behind; a crackling noise; shouts; a woman's scream. Andrew raced ahead.

His lungs were heaving by the time he reached the trees. He cursed every cigarette he had ever smoked and resolved to give up the habit at once.

Through the trees, Andrew slowed momentarily at what he saw. Although Jack Scott's house was still in darkness, the other blazed with lights, while from the rear rose tall, spark-shooting flames.

The woman's scream had stopped, but there were still shouts, both male and female. The flames were causing the crackling.

Andrew picked up speed again.

He came to the paved area and ran across it to the carport. On opening the kitchen door, he was met by a wall of fire. He slammed the door and stepped back.

Beside him appeared Mrs. Maynard. She wore a robe. Her hair was streaming loose, her eyes were wide.

"Quick!" she gasped. "Help!"

"What's happened?"

"Something blew up. Kitchen's on fire. Whole house is going to burn down!"

Andrew snapped, "Where's the hose?"

"That's what I came out for, through the front way," the woman said. "It's over there."

Andrew ran to a large faucet. He wrenched it on and began to reel out the hose from its drum.

Mrs. Maynard said, "Mr. Harry, he's inside getting at the flames with an extinguisher." She turned to Jim Webber, who had just arrived. "The whole house is on fire!"

"Go next door," Andrew ordered. "Call the firehouse."

The old man panted, "We ain't got one."

"The whole house!" Mrs. Maynard cried, the words rising to a wail. "It'll burn to the ground!"

Andrew snarled, "Shut up and get out of the way."

"What?"

"Sit in that car."

"You can't order me around."

Jim Webber said, "God's sake, woman. Move over there."

Andrew went past them with the hose, which was shooting water. He pinched the end to increase the range of the jet.

"Jim," he said, "you open this door a crack. Enough for me to aim inside."

"Right you are, son," the old man said, his voice tight with excitement. He strode to the kitchen door and eased it two inches away from its frame.

Already the flames were less high and fierce than before. Above their crackle, Andrew could hear the hollow whistle of an extinguisher. He joined its work with the jet of water.

"Okay, Jim," he said, noting that the passage of air was giving the fire no help. "Open 'er wide."

Jim Webber pushed the door fully open and stepped hastily away from the belch of smoke and heat. "Jesus!"

Andrew soon saw that the flames already had all the oxygen they needed: the window had, of course, been blasted out. But the fire seemed to be localised and was giving way under the twin assaults.

Presently Andrew was able to step through the doorway onto the rubber tile floor. The water that covered it was steaming hot. The flames were now concentrated along the back wall.

"That you, Mrs. Maynard?" a voice called.

Looking in that direction, Andrew saw through the smoke a bulky shape that he recognised. He said, "It's me, Mr. Scott. Bailey."

"Thanks for your help."

"My pleasure."

They were both shouting to be heard above the hiss and rumble, though standing no more than ten feet away from each other.

Another sound, from outside, came to Andrew clearly. It was the squeal of brakes. He turned his head to call, "Who's that, Jim?"

"Neighbours. Two trucks. And here comes another. The bang must've been heard for quite a ways."

Andrew passed that on to Harry Scott, who said a cheerful "Maybe we should've waited."

"Glad you're taking it so well."

"The place is insured and nobody's hurt. The rest, it's just inconvenience."

Andrew asked, "Where's your wife?"

"Her room. I told her to wait there. I knew there was no chance of the fire spreading."

Two big men lumbered into the room from outside, each carrying a fire extinguisher. One man, before the attack on the flames was joined, asked laconically, "Got any weenies, Harry?"

Twenty minutes later the scene had shifted houses, to Jack Scott's kitchen. It wasn't unlike the end of a barbecue, what with the smoke-smudged faces and smell of cooking. Mrs. Maynard was fixing bacon sandwiches to go with the coffee being passed out by Jim Webber.

There were upward of fifteen people in the room, some of them women. Andrew had been introduced around but hadn't managed to retain a single name. The gathering was boisterous, with one exception.

Elaine Scott, face pale, sat apart and silent. She looked, Andrew thought, as if the worst had happened and her home had burned to the foundations. She was watching the others with an expression that seemed part resentment, part envy.

"A pressure cooker," Harry said again. It was his second post-mortem. "A damn pressure cooker."

Mrs. Maynard looked around from the stove to say, as before, "I'm *sure* I turned the gas off before I went to bed."

Harry: "Don't give it another thought."

A man said, "But them things isn't supposed to explode. They have a safety valve. Right, Marge?"

The woman addressed shook her head scornfully. "They can jam, I guess. Same as any of these gimmicky things. Nothing's foolproof."

"Heard this great boom," Harry Scott said. "The bed danced a jig. I leapt up and threw on a few clothes and ran out. First I looked in Elaine's room, but she was okay, just getting up. So I ran on to the kitchen. It was burning as nice as you please."

A man said around a mouthful of bacon sandwich, "You should never have tried tackling it yourself, Harry. You should've called someone else first. It could've gotten out of hand."

Some of the neighbours took up the same refrain, while others laughed. Andrew put down his coffee cup and moved over to where Mrs. Scott sat. He sank to his haunches, asking, "Are you feeling better now? Less shaken?"

She inclined her head. "Thank you, yes."

"It was quite a blast."

"Harry's more rattled than I am."

"I think you're right. In my experience, overtalk is a symptom of shock."

Elaine Scott said, "Could be relief."

Andrew raised his eyebrows. "Moving to a different worry, you mean, away from the one over you?".

"Exactly."

The reliving of the event was still going on. Mrs. Maynard

shook her head as she continued frying bacon. Jim Webber looked like the owner of a successful snack bar.

Andrew asked, "Mrs. Scott, will this mean you'll have to move out of the house?"

The woman set her blond hair swinging. "Harry says he'll get men on the job at first light. It could be ready for new equipment within a couple of days. Perhaps three. Meanwhile, Mrs. Maynard can use this kitchen."

"But things are going to be pretty much in a turmoil."

"Yes."

"That lie-detector test," Andrew said. "Maybe we should postpone it until later."

Elaine Scott said, "Thank you. That would be best. I'll be worn out tomorrow."

"There's plenty of time."

Harry Scott was saying, "A damn pressure cooker."

FOUR

*Frost everywhere. It's worse than snow because it only
dabs whiteness here and there, leaving the rest in
dreary contrast to the sparkle. This is only the beginning. There's months of it ahead, getting colder every
day, just as the other thing is getting stronger. If it's not
my imagination. But a nice thought is that everything
might be cleared up by the sun, problems dissolved
with the snow. Nice, but a childish hope. It's the quiet
and steady sureness of it that's worst, most depressing.
It would be far better if it were all passion and shouting. He was so kind to me today I could have wept. In
fact, tears did come into my eyes. He saw them and
asked what was wrong. Highly concerned. I told him it
was because of having heard the church clock striking.
You could just hear it, luckily, floating over the still,
cold air. He laughed and called me a silly romantic. It
made me unsure of my ideas all over again. I guess I
should snoop more. Odious thought. What I should do
more of is keep myself busier, give my mind other di-
mensions, then I wouldn't be locked up with this thing
so much. It was good yesterday going to see the neighbours' new baby. What an angel he is. One's inclined to
forget all the pain involved, seeing only the sweetness
and innocence. That they should die, those entities, is
sad. How I always fought against the end of innocence
and faith in people. I'm still fighting, because not every-*

one by a long way is bad. There are merely a lot of rot-
ten apples, that's all, and some only in patches. Which
can be cured. Like a sickness. One that could, I sup-
pose, come back again sometime, but then so could the
cure. As the adage has it, honesty is the best policy.
Without a moral code, there's no point in anything. I do
lie once in a while, but the lies're white or pale grey.
Like the other night when I said I was unwell. It wasn't
true, the curse had gone, but I could sense that he did
it because he thought it was expected of him. So there
was a lie with an unselfish purpose. Unselfish? Well, not
altogether, I must admit that. Am I capable of pretend-
ing through the ultimate in intimacy? I doubt it. Yet I'll
have to sooner or later, unless I want to use a long-term
lie. Which, of course, would raise all manner of compli-
cations, all kinds of additional untruths and schemings.
The rolling snowball that gets bigger and bigger. I
couldn't stand it. . . .

"I didn't expect to hear from you this morning," Ann said
into the receiver. "At any rate. Don't tell me you had another midnight caller."

"Nothing so peaceful as that," Andrew said. "Has John
got there yet?"

"No, but he developed the automatic-writing pictures last
night and left the prints on my desk. The ones of Elaine in
her trance are very impressive."

"How about the pictures of the script?"

"Came out fine. I'm still doing a deciphering job. I'm getting it all, except for a few unimportant words, prepositions
and so on."

"Good. I'll get back to that in a minute. First, when John
appears, tell him not to come out here after all. The lie-detector test's been put off."

"Why's that?" Ann asked. She listened, and in each of Andrew's pauses she said, "My God." Her last comment was a jealousy-tinged "What a night."

"And when I got home, I accidentally tripped the camera that John had set up."

"Pardon me if I laugh."

"Go ahead. I'm not expecting any more visitors of that ilk. Tell John he can have his camera back."

"Okay," Ann said. "Have you got last night's writing?"

"Yes, but I haven't read it yet. Rennie Bates just dropped a copy off here. She'll be stopping by HQ with a copy as well, since she has to go into the city anyway."

"That's very sweet of her."

"Seriously, Ann, get chatty with Rennie. See if you can learn anything about the situation in general out this way."

"Will do."

"I'll get back to you as soon as I've read the latest instalment."

Ann put down the receiver and went back to work. She was still making a longhand translation of Elaine Scott's scrawl when the lab technician arrived. She said:

"Be with you in five minutes. But don't plan on going out to Hamlyn Creek. The lie test is off."

John Bright smoothed a hand over his baldness. "That I find real interesting."

"Good. Now scat."

John went whistling into the laboratory and Ann continued with her work. She interrupted herself only to glance at the telephone, expecting Andrew's call at any moment and hoping it wouldn't come until she had got through with the deciphering, so that she could discuss it with him.

There was no call. Relieved, Ann finished the script and read it twice. The most intriguing part was in the first half, up to the metaphor of the rolling snowball. After that, it maundered in and around the weather and its effect on the scenery.

Ann got up and went into the laboratory, announcing, "I hate this place."

"That's my girl," John Bright said. He was busy at a bench. "Like to see some pretty fingerprints?"

"Not terribly, thanks. Like to read the new piece of automatic writing?"

"Can't wait. For more than a few hours. But tell me about the cancelled date."

Ann explained about the fire at the Scotts' house. The story was received with a laugh. John Bright said, "Surprise, surprise."

"Meaning, I imagine, that you think the explosion was a deliberate act."

"I do."

"That it was worth causing hundreds of dollars' worth of damage to the kitchen and destroying appliances, to say nothing of mess and inconvenience."

"I do, I do."

Ann said, "To delay the inevitable, the lie-detector test? Really, John. That's making a fetish of cynicism."

The lab man waved his finger like a metronome. "Don't forget how rich these people are. The fire to them is like someone else allowing a roast to burn."

"Yesterday you were saying the Scotts were phonying this affair for the money. Make up your mind."

John Bright shrugged cheerfully. He was used to stalemate in his exchanges with Ann. The dogma on either side was logic-proof.

Ann looked at her wristwatch. "I'm surprised Andrew hasn't called back by now."

"When he does," John said, "tell him that the prints on the lamp belong to Mrs. Maynard, Mr. and Mrs. Scott, and other unknown persons. On the rocking chair: Andrew's, Mrs. Maynard's, the Scott brothers', Elaine's, and one other unidentified person."

"Seems to me," Ann said, "that you've got too many prints to be any good, and all the expected ones at that."

Before John could answer, the doorbell rang. Ann went to let in the caller—Rennie Bates, who handed over an envelope and accepted gladly the offer of coffee: "The heater in that old crate of mine's always on the bum."

Ann put her into an easy chair and went upstairs to Andrew's kitchen. As usual she was piqued that the place wasn't a shambles, crying out for a woman's touch. She dropped two spoons and a dish towel and forgot to pick them up.

When Ann went downstairs, carrying a tray, she saw that the lab technician was playing host and that the visitor was playing coy.

Rennie Bates touched her boyish hair. "I'm so glad you like it, John. I wasn't real sure about this style."

"It's great. Fabulous. Suits you."

Ann said, "It reminds me of Mary's." She added to the visitor, "That's the oldest of John's three children."

"Thanks for bringing that up," John said, smiling. "It was the opportunity I was looking for." He winked at her covertly to show that he was serious, while bringing out his billfold and handing it over.

Ann sighed. She was tempted to say, "Why don't you simply ask her if you can take her fingerprints? This is an investigation, after all." But the ploy was soon done, and John excused himself to go back to his work.

The two girls passed the time of day over coffee and cookies. Ann found Rennie Bates easy to talk to. There was no need to fish, beyond:

"I'll admit, Rennie, to being wildly intrigued with the Scotts and this whole situation."

"That makes two of us. The situation, anyway. This writing thing is the weirdest. Especially as it's happened to Elaine. I mean, she's so down to earth you wouldn't believe it."

"I must say that in spite of what's going on she did strike me as being the ultrasensible type."

That led to a dissection of character. It was a little spiteful, a mite envious, a measure superior (they were both younger than Elaine), and very normal. Ann enjoyed it.

She said, "Basically tough, though. Must be to have come through that murder thing unscathed." If, she added to herself, she has. "What happened that night exactly?"

Rennie Bates, keen, gulped a mouthful of biscuit. "I was at the inquest, y'know. Everyone was that could get in. It caused quite a local stir."

"I can imagine."

"Elaine described the event so vividly you could almost see it, the car in the trees and the two of them dressed up in white. Anyway, Elaine left Cissy and went on foot to the farmhouse—a couple of hundred yards. She had a basket of goodies with her. Near the house, by a tractor, she thought she heard a movement and turned quickly. She hit the back of her head on the tractor's side. She nearly went back to Cissy. Just think of that."

"No, thanks. I've got goose bumps already."

"She might've saved Cissy or they could both have been killed."

"Yes, but what happened?"

"In the house Elaine stayed only ten minutes. I guess there was so much racket, kids and all, that it drowned out the gunshots. She was about to leave, they were seeing her off, when she noticed that the trees were dark. Before, the car lights had been on. The others went with her—and they found Cissy."

Ann shuddered. "How awful. And it was their own gun."

"You just never know what's going to happen to you," Rennie Bates said. "I'll tell you, it was a big relief when they put that boy away."

"And they say cities are dangerous."

"Which reminds me. I have things to do in the metropolis."

Another minute, and Ann was ushering the visitor out. As she closed the door, John Bright came from his room. He said, "You might care to know that the other prints on the chair belong to Miss Rennie Bates."

"Hardly surprising. She was there that same evening. She probably sat in that rocker."

"You mean she and Andrew sat in it together? Mmm. You could have something there."

"Talking of Andrew," Ann said. She looked at her watch. "I wonder what . . ."

The telephone rang. Ann strode to her desk and picked up the receiver. She smiled. "Oh, good. I couldn't think what had happened to you."

"I came to the village. I'm calling from the drugstore."

"Okay," Ann said. "Listen." She gave Andrew the information on the fingerprints and, as close to verbatim as she could remember, told of her talk with Rennie Bates.

Slowly, Andrew said, "I see, I see."

"Hey, that's your secret-keeping voice, if I'm not mistaken."

He became brisk. "You are. I have news. But first, what d'you think of the latest writing?"

"Well," Ann said, "it's the mixture as before but a bit stronger. The foreboding, the depression, everything on the downbeat. Also, there's more of what looks now like domestic squabbling."

Andrew said, "Yes, and a couple of other things. For one, the scripts are set pretty firmly at one time of year, the autumn."

"Not just winter?"

"No, fall. She talks of the cold ahead. But that's not the big news in this latest work."

"The news is big?" Ann asked, and she could almost see Andrew giving one of his emphatic nods. He said:

"That's the reason I came to the Creek. I had a nice long chat with an official in the township office. A very helpful young man. He was delighted when I showed an interest in Hamlyn Creek's history."

"Are you going to draw this out forever, Andrew?"

"No. Listen. The script mentions menstruation. It also mentions hearing the church clock striking. And guess what?"

"Please, Andrew."

"That clock was installed when Moina O'Neal was, by my reckoning, fifty-nine years old."

Ann shaped her mouth to say an "Oh" but nothing came out.

"And fifty-nine," Andrew said, "is long past menopause. Agreed?"

"Agreed."

"Therefore, whoever the writing is coming from, it is not coming from Moina O'Neal."

Andrew strolled along the main street of Hamlyn Creek. He was pleased. He had enjoyed the admiration in Ann's voice when she complimented him on his thoroughness and attention to detail.

Andrew was forced to admit to himself now, however,

that it was Jim Webber's passing reference to the church clock that had given him the idea of checking out that angle. But he hadn't said so to Ann.

Andrew resolved to correct the omission as soon as possible. And he would keep the resolution, he thought. He always did.

After lighting a cigarette, Andrew went through a doorway and up a flight of bare wooden stairs. The door he stopped at said J. Scott, General Broker. He tapped, then obeyed a call to enter.

The office was severely functional and free of clutter. From behind the one desk rose Jack Scott. He looked, Andrew mused, slightly embarrassed, like a boy caught in the act of positioning a stool under the cookie jar.

"Am I interrupting anything?" Andrew asked.

"Hell, no. I'm just holding down Rennie's post till she gets back. If anyone comes here on business, I won't know where to start."

"This is a hobby first, a job second?"

"Right on, Mr. Bailey," Jack Scott said. "In fact, I believe I'll quit and go out to the course."

"What's your handicap?"

They spent some minutes talking golf. Andrew, a player himself, recognised the other man's fanaticism, the essence that would make him good, seeing the game as a personal challenge rather than a pastime.

Andrew said, "Well, I won't detain you. I only stopped by to see what was new on the fire."

Jack Scott came around the desk. "Not a thing. Harry has workmen in there tearing the place apart."

"As your brother said, it's the inconvenience as much as anything."

"True. Even so, it's real odd."

"Odd?"

"Pressure cookers have been known to blow up," Jack Scott said. "But it rarely happens. It's as rare as a computer making a mistake."

Andrew said, "Well now, I don't know about that. Our last telephone bill was for over three million dollars. A few extra zeroes got in there somehow."

They laughed. Jack Scott went to a corner and hefted a golf bag. He asked, "Read Elaine's latest effort yet? Haven't had the time myself."

"Yes," Andrew said. "Pretty similar to the others."

"No mention of those sovereigns?"

"No mention of anything really."

"Oh well."

The men went downstairs together. Out on the street Andrew asked, "If it wasn't a pressure cooker, what was it?"

"Oh, I guess it's just me and my fail-safe thing. Don't give it another thought. See you."

Back at his car, Andrew got in beside the black box on the passenger seat. He had put it there because he felt it was safer with him than left at his temporary home.

The next three hours Andrew spent driving around the area and stopping off at farms and country stores. Most people were those whose names he had gotten from old Jim Webber. Andrew didn't feel that he was wasting his time, though he did bid a regretful semi-farewell to his theory on sociobiology, at least as it related here.

Stopping at a coffee shop attached to a gas station, Andrew lunched on two hamburgers.

Nearing the O'Neal place, he slowed on passing a clump of trees. The ground rose in the middle, so that the nearby farmhouse was out of sight. Andrew recalled what Ann had told him on the telephone of her talk with Rennie Bates. He too could almost see the pair of figures in white costumes.

He drove on, went past the gatehouse and along to the

twin houses, which he circled. There he halted. Getting out, he crossed a lawn to the gaping black hole that had been a window. On the grass lay a mess of scorched and buckled kitchen equipment, and another piece flew out of the window as Andrew stopped.

Inside, male voices and sounds of action ended on Andrew's shout of "Hold it!"

Harry Scott looked out. He was grimy but cheerful— cheerful until the exchange of greetings was over, when Andrew asked, "How's Mrs. Scott today?"

Scott frowned. "Not too good. A bit nervous. None of this has helped, of course."

"Of course not."

"And she's had another session of her writing."

"That's fast work."

"I tried to call you at the old place but there was no answer."

"I was in the village."

Harry gave a glum nod. "When I have a minute, I'll call Rennie to come and get the script."

"Give it to me," Andrew said quickly. "I'm used to the writing now. I'll soon figure it out. In any case, Rennie's in Toronto."

Harry Scott hesitated, shrugged, turned away. "Hold on."

His place at the window was taken by a man in a red baseball cap. He dropped an armful of twisted wires outside. Andrew asked him, "Where's the pressure cooker?"

"Somewhere in that lot, I guess, but in a thousand and one itty-bitty pieces."

Andrew nodded. He looked among the rubble until Harry Scott returned and handed out two pieces of paper. "It was a short one."

"Doesn't matter if it's only a few lines."

"Another thing. Elaine says she'll be okay to take that test in the morning. Would eleven be all right?"

Andrew didn't smile until he was back at the car.

He drove on but soon slowed on seeing Mrs. Maynard ahead. She was walking this way, waddling in a heavy top-coat. When she had come abreast of the car, Andrew braked.

The woman said promptly, "I've just been to the old house." There was in her manner a touch of the bellicose, and Andrew wondered if it could be because he had spoken to her sharply last night, or perhaps because he'd seen her distraught. "I left you that recipe you asked for and a wedge of a cake I baked this morning."

"Very kind of you, ma'am."

She settled that with "Mrs. Scott said you might care for something sweet."

Andrew smiled forgivingly, which made the woman snap her gaze away. She made as though to walk on. Andrew said:

"Tell me, ma'am. What do you think of the writing that's being done by your employer?"

Still looking away, Mrs. Maynard said flatly, "It's rubbish."

"Then you don't believe she really goes into trances?"

Now she did look at him—hotly. "She's not pretending, if that's what you mean. Trance, faint, sleep, call it what you want. It's real. I reckon it's a way of escaping."

Andrew nodded slowly, respectfully. He asked, "And what would she be escaping from, ma'am?"

"Boredom. The poor girl needs something to do with her life. She sits and reads, or writes poetry, or looks out of the window. Plenty of time for that when she's fifty years older. She's far too young to . . ."

There was more. Nor did it end as Mrs. Maynard, blinking by way of farewell, left and went on toward the houses. Andrew drove off.

At the old homestead, after calling headquarters with word of the lie-detector test, Andrew set to work on decoding the two pieces of paper. On a separate pad he wrote down every word as it became clear. With some checking against previous scripts, he had the job done in fifteen minutes.

He read through the translation. At once he noted an increase in the feeling of tension. There was haste. The sentences were short and clipped. It was the work of someone in a hurry, Andrew thought.

On a separate page he rewrote what he considered to be the pertinent sections. These were:

It's clear now what's going on. Been going on for some time. I've been fooling myself. But I still can't believe it. You only read about these things. And even then you don't accept them as real.

More proof. I don't need to look any more. It keeps hitting me in the face. But he goes on smiling. The world is fine and bright. It's unbearable. How can I go on? But I must, and without letting it show that I know. That's the hardest of all.

It's all around me, this atmosphere. So far it's defied definition. All I know is, it's unpleasant, alien. It makes me want to turn to someone for help.

After putting this page in his pocket, Andrew started again to write out the script. But now he put in every innocuous detail and left out the pertinent sections.

Finished, he took the original two pieces of paper and locked them in his suitcase for later photographing and filing.

It was dark when Andrew had finished his supper of warmed-up stew and a slice of Mrs. Maynard's cake. He put on his coat and went out to the car.

The track he steered onto led out the other side of the old homestead's cluster of clapboard buildings. It brought him, after about a mile, to what could have passed for a village of the future: an essay in concrete and steel. This was the modern core of the O'Neal spread.

There was no one about, no lights showing. Andrew got out with his flashlight and went to the nearest building. Its door was unlocked, as were all the others he subsequently tried.

Taking his time, Andrew poked about. He looked at the monsters of field equipment, tapped his foot against a drum of kerosene, shook his head in mystification at objects whose function was beyond his ken.

He returned to the car and drove on. As he had known, the track eventually led him to a public road, the edge of the estate. He circled to its main entrance and stopped at the gatehouse.

Jim Webber was delighted at the visit and the prospect of a game of cribbage. He said, "Come on in, son."

When they were sitting in the high-backed chairs the old man shuffled the pack and then fanned it out. "Take a card, any card, and I'll tell you what it is."

Andrew selected. He was surprised when old Jim said, "It's the ace of clubs."

"Hey, that's pretty clever."

"A setup," the host said sheepishly. "And I made it that one because it's you."

"The ace of clubs is me?"

"Sure. I see the cards as people sometimes, a-settin' here. For instance, Tom Stamford, the local cop, he's the ace of diamonds. Number one and real sharp."

"Thanks for giving me a one as well," Andrew said. "But what's my club stand for?"

"Solid and respectable," the old man said. "Harry Scott now, he's the two of hearts. Not quite the best, and real sentimental."

"How about Rennie Bates?"

"The girl ain't fully developed yet in character. I've given her a three of diamonds to be going on with."

"Haig Wilson?" Andrew asked, intrigued with this idea.

The old man said, "A heart, on account of he's a heartthrob, or reckons he is. And I set him at number four."

"Jack Scott?"

"Another ace of diamonds. And there's that fussy Maynard woman as I wouldn't let a yard near my kitchen. She's a three of spades. Pale ones."

"How does Mrs. Scott rate?"

The old man smiled fondly. "Ah now, she's an ace, a real ace, and I make it hearts because that's the royal one. Cissy too. I reckoned her the same, always. A couple of princesses. Nothing worse could've happened to anyone nicer."

Andrew nodded encouragement, and while Jim Webber talked of the tragedy of last year he listened patiently, though he heard nothing new.

He picked up the deck of cards and shuffled. "Let's have some action, Jim. Drive away the cold. It's bitter tonight."

"Well, fall's getting on, y'know," the old man said. "Halloween is right around the corner."

"Would you tell me your name, please."

"Elaine Mary Scott."

"Is it raining?"

"No."

"Have you been married ten years?"

"Last April 14, yes."

"Are you wearing a green dress?"

"You could call it green."

Except for the voices of Elaine Scott and John Bright, the living room was quiet. Andrew, who was still getting used to the faint smell of smoke, stood out of the way by a window, the silent observer. He was the only one not actively involved. Harry Scott had been sent away by his wife, who had said he made her nervousness worse.

Not, Andrew mused, that she looked particularly nervous. In fact she was calmer than he had ever seen her. Though "lifeless" would have been a better word. Depleted through resignation or defeat, exhaustion or ennui.

Elaine was sitting head back in an easy chair, her vacant gaze fixed on the mantelpiece. Circling her chest, neck and upper arm were bands, from which cables fed back behind the chair to the coffee table on which John Bright had set up his equipment.

Andrew, who had used lie detectors during his days as a police officer, would have liked to conduct this test himself. But he was willing to give in to John's superior knowledge and experience.

The technician finished with his preliminary questions: subject was reacting normally, the needle making the appropriate scrawls on the slowly moving graph.

John Bright said, "You have been producing what is assumed to be automatic writing, Mrs. Scott. Is that correct?"

"It is."

"Are you happy about that?"

"Not particularly," the blond woman said, her voice as low on animation as her appearance.

"Are you aware of what you are doing during these writing sessions?"

"I am not."

Andrew had positioned himself so that he could see the

graph. Its needle's dither remained constant, and again when John rephrased the same question:

"Do you realise that you are writing?"

"I do not."

John Bright, who was making a note of each question asked in order to match the graph, said, "Has this ever happened to you before, at any time in your life?"

"No, never. I don't understand it."

"Just answer the questions, please."

"Sorry."

"Do you have any history of sleepwalking?"

"No."

"Lapse of memory?"

"No."

"Emotional disturbance?"

Shaking her head fractionally, Elaine Scott said with a trace of impatience, "No. Nothing like that. No."

The needle was steady.

"Mrs. Scott," the lab man said, "would you lie?"

There was a pause, the needle moved slightly out of line, and the woman said, "Yes, of course I would. We all tell lies."

"Have you been lying in any way about the trances?"

"No."

Needle steady.

John Bright firmed his voice and began to put his questions at a faster pace. "Were you fond of your grandmother?"

"Yes."

"Do you love your husband?"

"Very much."

"Would you like this test to stop?"

"Yes."

"Why?"

"Being grilled is unpleasant."

"Are you afraid of this investigation?"

"Not in the least."

"Are you concerned about the trances?"

"Yes."

"Tell me why, please."

"I don't like them," Elaine Scott said tonelessly. "I don't understand them. They're out of my control."

Andrew looked away from the graph, which had recorded in the subject's favour throughout, and took a step from the window. He asked in a casual voice:

"If you're not afraid of the investigation, Mrs. Scott, what are you afraid of?"

It was, he knew, an improper question; meaning that it was unanswerable with a simple affirmative or negative. But John Bright had already asked two of the same kind, and the value of a lie detector went beyond that. It showed reactions to hints, sounds, sights, sensations.

Now the needle was fluctuating. The woman had brought her gaze lower, at the same time easing her head off the chair back. She said, "The trances. I told you. I'm afraid of the trances."

"Concerned, you said."

"*He* said. Concerned is putting it mildly. It's terrifying not to be in control of yourself."

"Is there something else you're afraid of?"

The woman said, "Everything connected with the trances."

"Were you afraid when there was that explosion in the kitchen?"

"Of course."

Andrew asked, "You didn't know what it was?"

"At that moment, no," Elaine Scott said, putting her head back. "Not the slightest idea."

The needle had returned to steady.

Andrew, signalling to John to continue, moved to a chair and sat down. He wasn't sure, but he had the feeling that he had been outmaneuvered.

With the graph remaining normal, the questioning went on.

No, neither she nor the Scott brothers were short of money. Yes, the farm was highly successful. She wasn't sure whether or not she believed in the supernatural. Yes, she thought her verses were good but doubted if anyone else would. No, she didn't smoke, gave it up two years ago with the help of hypnotism. No, she didn't want to be famous. Yes, she would be unhappy if this affair got into the newspapers.

Elaine Scott sat up. She said, "Could we finish now, please? I'm rather tired."

"Certainly," Andrew said. "You've been very patient."

While John Bright was removing the bands from her body, the woman said, "I think I'm entitled to ask you a question, Mr. Bailey."

"I agree. Go ahead."

"In my grandmother's sewing room. That ensemble of nightgown, chair, and lamp. Did you honestly not put them there?"

Andrew shook his head. "I had nothing to do with it."

"Well, do you know what it signified?"

"Probably that someone has a cute sense of humour."

"I see."

In five minutes the men were ready to leave. Andrew indicated a table. "On there is an envelope, Mrs. Scott. It holds my transcription of your writing of last night."

The woman closed her eyes on a nod. "Thank you."

Outside, in the car, John Bright turned from putting his case on the back seat to ask a heavy "Well?"

"Except for the trances being not of her volition, I'd say the test was inconclusive."

"That or she's one clever lady."

Andrew started the car and steered around the houses. "Someone's clever," he said. He got out cigarettes, offered the pack.

Taking one, John said, "Which reminds me. That butt you gave me to run a test on. It's months old."

Andrew grinned cheerfully. "That's fine. Good old process of elimination. The case moves."

"But in which direction?"

"At this stage I wouldn't care to venture a guess."

The lab man looked at him closely. "You know more than you're pretending, Chief."

"Balls. All I know is I have lots of ideas."

"Listen. Why don't we use the black box on everyone involved in this deal?"

Stopping the Ford beside John's car near the homestead porch, Andrew said, "Because they wouldn't go for it, and we might get the push. I'd hate that. I'm intrigued as hell."

They went inside. After dismantling his trip camera and declining a slice of cake, John Bright set off to drive back to the city.

Andrew lunched on cake and coffee before going into the sewing room. He spent an hour diligently going through the papers, letters, and diaries of Moina O'Neal. All her business dealings were recorded, down to how much she had paid for the stitching on a set of harness.

Stiff from sitting, Andrew went out and strolled for a while in the bright, sharp outdoors. He felt like walking more but there were things to do.

He drove to town, parked, and asked a passer-by for directions. The house he found without trouble. The doctor was on his way out, with his wife, and fretted at the delay. But when Andrew had explained his mission the doctor didn't balk at discussing his patient—in general terms. He gave Elaine Scott a clean bill of health. His wife said, "I should be so fit."

Andrew turned back, crossed the main street and went on walking. He liked the way the huge old trees grew insolently a yard out from the kerbstones. Red and yellow leaves lay everywhere.

When the township's buildings were dwindling, Andrew came to a barn. It was painted a startling orange and black. A sign said: Hamlyn Creek Little Theatre.

The posters announcing the last play were tattered and weather-white, and Andrew recalled hearing that the amateur group put on only four productions a year.

He tried the door beside the box-office window. It was locked. Going around to the side of the barn, he found another door. It gave when he pushed. Feeling like a trespasser, he went in as quietly as if the place were a church.

He was in a dim passage which led away from the front. He followed, treading softly. He stopped on hearing voices. They were faint: a man and a woman talking. Though the words were not clear, the tone was unmistakably confidential.

Andrew went on again. His step was quieter than before. He did nothing to disturb the silence that gave a slight echo to the pair of voices.

In front of him was a door, standing six inches ajar, with brightness coming through the opening. The voices had grown louder. The female was saying, "I don't believe you know what the word 'love' means."

The male laughed and said, "You're teasing."

Andrew stopped by the door. Through its opening he could see the talkers. They were facing him, sitting on the apron of a stage that was bare save for hampers. The man was Haig Wilson; the girl was Rennie Bates.

She said, smiling, "Could you ever, really, accuse me of being a tease?"

"I wasn't talking about things physical, my dear."

"From you, that's a nice change."

"You make me sound like the biggest wolf in the world," Haig Wilson said. He raised a hand and rested it on the girl's shoulder.

She said, "You are. That's why I fell for you."

"Lower your voice, angel."

"What on earth for? No one can hear us out here, fifty miles from the nearest smell of civilisation."

Haig Wilson said, "Amen to that."

"And look at the moon, the way it lives again in the river."

"The way we will live again."

Andrew scuffled his feet, coughed, and opened the door. The actors looked his way mildly. Not so forgiving was a man who rose into view from between the blocks of seating.

Short, stout, and middle-aged, with raging white hair like a conductor, he stared at Andrew and asked icily, "Just who might you be, sir?"

Slipping off the stage, Rennie Bates went to his side. "It's okay, Claud. This is someone who's staying with the Scotts." She made the introductions.

Claud Trubolt became affable. Directing was his hobby, he explained, amplifying the introduction. He was a retired merchant who, in his youth, had been on the professional stage. By the grand way he talked of those days, Andrew judged him to have carried a short spear off Broadway.

"Claud," Haig Wilson said with hammy patience, "it's no use buttering up Mr. Bailey. He can't influence Elaine's subsidy."

"In any case," Rennie said, "I'm sure she'll give it as usual."

The director looked confused. He laughed, stammered, shook hands with Andrew and went up into the wings where a man was staring at a can of paint.

The actors both turned to Andrew with questioning expressions. He said, "No, nothing special. I simply stopped by because I'm naturally nosy."

They asked about the latest on the fire and on the automatic writing. After answering, Andrew asked why Rennie wasn't at the office—"Took the whole day off"—and how Haig and his guest had enjoyed the wrestling—"Old Jack, he isn't enjoying anything much these days."

"But he does try," the girl said. "Don't give up on him, Haig."

"Hell, no."

"Look how he put on that happy face when Harry bought them a new tape deck apiece."

Andrew smiled. "Identical, of course."

Nodding, Rennie Bates said, "You never would've guessed that he didn't give a damn."

The sports writer said, "Give Harry credit, he goes to a lot of trouble to take the weight off his kid brother."

"They're close, those two. I like to see that."

Andrew asked the reporter, "You've known the Scotts a long time?"

"All my life. We were kids here together."

"And Cissy?"

"Only since she married Jack. He imported her from Toronto. But she took to the country real well, without sinking into a rut. She livened us all up."

"Started this theatre group," Rennie said. "She was the star and driving force. Me, I'm failing miserably at taking her place as leading female light."

Haig Wilson began to argue with her on that point. She put up barriers that were made of feathers.

From outside came the sound of a car horn. The girl said, "That'll be my date. Must dash, boys."

Haig tutted. "Too old for you, cutie. He must be all of twenty-three."

Rennie Bates laughed, grabbed a blanket-thick cardigan off a seat, shouted good-byes and hurried out. Andrew said he would have to be going as well. Wilson said the same. They left together, after an elaborate farewell from Claud Trubolt, who called a final "Do give my very fondest regards to Elaine, Mr. Bailey."

Andrew felt puny beside the husky sports writer as they strolled along the street. He asked, "So you would say that Cissy Scott was happy in the sticks?"

"I sure would. She almost glowed. A vital woman. She made everyone feel more alive."

"And feel her death all the more."

"Right. Absolutely right. Poor old Jack, you can't blame him if he ties one on occasionally."

"I didn't know he was a big drinker."

Haig Wilson sent a pile of leaves aloft with a kick. "He's not. Never was. But this past year he's had one or two quiet, morose benders."

"It can be a help."

"After the wrestling the other night, we sank more than a few. Then we drank coffee until three in the morning, so we could drive."

"Well, at least Jack's being sensible."

"Always was. Harry's the dreamer."

Andrew asked, "Have you, by the way, actually read any of Elaine's scripts?"

"Couple," Haig Wilson said, again taking a kick at leaves.

"Stream-of-consciousness stuff. She probably has secret yearnings to switch from verse to prose."

"Well, that's a new angle, if nothing else."

They separated on the main street. Andrew got in his car and went out to the dirt roads. He called at a farm and a store, seeing people who had been unavailable the day before.

The sky was darkening when he got back to town. In a coffee shop he had a roast beef sandwich with gravy and mashed potatoes. The waitress asked him if he was that famous ghost catcher from the city. Andrew gave a modest nod, but the girl giggled.

Tipping small, Andrew left and drove off. He headed for the O'Neal place. Although he was not in the mood for anything as quiet as a game of cribbage, he stopped off at Jim Webber's. He stayed two hours, playing cards, asking casual questions about people past and present but then falling silent.

He went on to the old homestead. He was upstairs, beginning to undress, when he heard the telephone. He hurried down. The caller was Harry Scott, who said:

"Elaine's in a trance. I thought you'd like to know."

"Thanks. Be right with you."

"I tried to get you earlier—could tell a trance was coming on—but there was no answer."

"I've been at old Jim's."

"Oh?"

"I go there to get taught cribbage," Andrew said. "See you in five minutes."

It was less than that when he walked through the Scott kitchen, which was bright with fresh paint and new linoleum, though bare of fittings. He strode on to the living room.

Harry Scott was standing by the chair on which sat his

wife. Elaine's eyes were semi-closed, her pen-holding hand lay idle on the pad whose top page was covered part way down with writing.

Her husband whispered, "I think that's all. She looks to be coming out of it."

Andrew waited until Elaine Scott gave a long, shuddery sigh and stirred, before taking the pad and pulling off its top three, used pages, which he put in his pocket.

The woman lifted her head, looked around. She asked, "Where . . . ?"

"Good night to you both," Andrew said. He left quickly.

FIVE

Ann steered onto the cloverleaf. Below, off the underpass, was the restaurant where she was meeting Andrew for lunch. He hadn't been too definite on the telephone about why he wanted to meet here, halfway between the city and Hamlyn Creek, but apart from that he had been precise and keen.

Ann hoped she wasn't in for a session of facts and figures, plus physical evidence, the type of thing that John Bright would moon over but that sent her into depression. The case looked to be going that way.

Of course, Ann thought, at least there had been that cigarette-butt clue turning out to be a dud. It was something.

She drew up in front of the low, modern building that was all glass and aluminium, like a rest home for computers. Inside, she crossed the hushed lobby and went into the bar.

Andrew got off his stool. "You're not late," he said. "What's wrong?"

They kissed, and Ann told him, "Autumn fever." She patted his arm. "You're looking brimful of bloodhoundness."

"Or something. What's your drink?"

When they were sitting on stools and Ann had sipped at her sherry, Andrew put an envelope and a piece of paper on the bar. He said:

"The envelope's for your files. It has the original and the transcription of last night's automatic writing."

"Again? Last night?"

He nodded. "Thick and fast."

"I wonder why? If, as you believe, she's faking it."

"I didn't say that."

"You said it definitely wasn't Moina O'Neal, and I have to agree with you."

Andrew said, "More about that later." He tapped the piece of paper. "This has the pertinent matter from the new script. A doctored version of which I gave to the Scotts."

"So they don't know about these juicy bits?"

"They do not. And I hope to keep it that way, to go on doing this, if possible. I've been lucky so far. I feel I should be there at all times." He glanced over his shoulder. "I hate being even this far away."

Ann smiled. "Not very flattering to me, but I forgive you. I know how you feel."

"The reason we met here," Andrew said, "is because I'm getting a nice healthy paranoia about this case."

"Typical. You think everyone's after the secrets you're hogging. In my case, you're right."

"No, Ann, it's Hamlyn Creek and confines. I'm not even sure about the telephone being safe. Point is, everyone and his dog is a friend of the Scotts. The doctor's a second cousin, the mayor plays golf with Jack, the local cop once had a crush on Mrs. Scott."

"I see what you mean."

"But I have to stay close to the writing source," Andrew said. He took a quick drink of beer. "The ideal, of course, would be for me to move into the house."

"You could come up with some excuse to get invited in, surely."

"I haven't so far. And it's worse now that their kitchen's out of the running. Hardly a good time for guests."

"You could get sick," Ann said. She went on, warming to the idea, "Something that needn't keep you bedridden.

Elaine would probably be glad of the chance to play nurse. Give her something to do."

"It's a thought," Andrew agreed. "But let's get to the latest production. Read it, please." He folded his arms and closed his eyes. "Read it aloud. Let me hear how it sounds."

Ann put the envelope in her pocketbook and picked up the piece of paper. She read out:

"He's such a great person. A genuine and sweet person. It's hard to believe this is happening. Because of him and everything else. I stood today looking at the twin houses. Firm and solid. They make it all seem ridiculous."

Andrew said, "Next."

"The atmosphere. Or smell or aura or ambience, or whatever you like to call it. Except imagination. Which it isn't. Anyway, it's growing stronger. I can't see a connection."

His eyes still closed, Andrew said, "There it is again, the talk of an atmosphere. Something tells me it's important."

"It means nothing to me, Andrew. Unless it's a psychical sensation she's talking about."

"Go on, please."

Ann read aloud:

"Jack mustn't know, of course. I hope it can be kept from him. He's so straight. Everyone admires him. You can't say that about many businessmen. In the supermarket yesterday he shook hands a dozen times."

Andrew said promptly, "Last bit."

"If only I had someone to tell, talk to. I feel a
stranger here. I know hundreds of people but can I call
a single one friend? No. Everything's negative."

Ann put down the paper. "Well, the tone has certainly
changed."

As Andrew opened his eyes, a man sidled up like an un-
successful pickpocket to murmur, "Your table, Mr. Bailey."

They finished their drinks. Walking across the lobby to
the dining room, Andrew said, "It sounded better read by a
woman."

Ann held back her questions, nor did she quibble when, at
the table, Andrew suggested the menu of the day. It would
be faster. He was obviously in no mood for a meal taken at
leisure.

Waiter gone, Andrew said, "Yes, Ann, the tone of the
scripts is changing. This one's more personal. We have
names now, and places. Things are warming up."

"So are you," Ann said. "Try and relax."

He pointed to her purse. "The one who's dictating that
stuff. Any ideas?"

"You're the one in the field, not me, sad to say. But how
about Elaine's mother?"

"No. There's a mention of the twin houses. They were
after her time."

"Then there's only one strong candidate."

"Who's that?"

"Cissy Scott."

Andrew nodded. "Yes."

Ann raised her eyebrows in amusement. "But she's dead."

Irritably he said, "I know, I know. I'm not ruling out any
possibility. Not yet. I'm the one with the open mind, remember?"

"Of course, dear. I'm sorry. I'm also tickled pink."

He smiled, abashed. "I'm not at my charming best today."

Ann reached over and pressed his hand. "You're marvellous. This is a moment I'm going to remember."

"I'll improve it for you," Andrew said. He told about the lie-detector test, finishing, "On one point, though, it was clear. John agrees with me on it, too. The trances seem to be not of Elaine's making."

"Genuine, then?"

"I won't commit myself that far. There could be other causes apart from the paranormal."

"I don't know of any."

"In their living room last night," Andrew said, "the TV was on, though Harry had turned the sound down. And you know, of course, what a flickering light can produce."

Ann nodded. "I'd forgotten. They say that one person in four is a potential epileptic, from the mildest form upward. He might go all his life without knowing it, but it only needs his personal light pattern to send him into a seizure."

"Exactly. But I've never heard of anyone writing in petit mal."

"Thank you, dear."

The waiter came and started serving. Andrew's intake of soup was limited to three spoonfuls. After that he lit a cigarette. Ann, amenable, put down her spoon. She said:

"All right. Cissy Scott. Elaine's sister-in-law. She's not happy. There's an atmosphere she doesn't understand or like. She suspects some kind of intrigue, and the one who's involved in that is a male."

"In a nutshell, Ann. So who is the man and what is the intrigue?"

"A skeleton in the Scott family closet, maybe. Or something from her pre-Hamlyn Creek days."

Andrew shook his head firmly. "No. Again there's the twin houses mentioned."

"Well, let's think."

They were silent until the main course had been served. Picking without interest at the steak and kidney pie, Andrew said, "My mind's a blank."

Ann didn't believe him. She said nevertheless, "Don't worry, so is mine."

"Tell you what, though. I have the same feeling I've had all along. Which is that in some way we're being used."

Ann pointed out, "You've said the same thing on other cases."

"Yes, and often I've been wrong. Sometimes, however, I was right. Remember the Tyler business?"

Until the waiter came back they discussed that and other cases. Andrew declined dessert. Ann, thinking that you could take being amenable to absurd lengths, ordered the banana cream pie.

Andrew said, "Don't forget to show the latest transcription to John."

Ann nodded. "He didn't come in this morning, by the way."

"I know. I called him at home early. He's out in the country somewhere playing boy scout."

"Mm?"

"He's building a fire under a pressure cooker."

Ann swallowed pie. "Seriously?"

"Yes. I hope he was able to buy one wholesale."

Ann sighed. "So you haven't given up on the possibility of fraud, it seems."

"Open mind, Ann. Open mind."

"Yes, Mr. Bailey."

"You can also ask John if he has any ideas on how to get me into the Scott house. I'm scared of scripts going astray, so to speak."

"Check," Ann said. "No jobs for me?"

"As a matter of fact I have. I want you to go to one of the city newspapers and look in their morgue. Get details on Cissy Scott's death."

Ann nodded. "I'll do that. You know, I'm beginning to feel as excited as you are."

Andrew looked at his watch. He asked, "Would you hate me if I split?"

"Under these promising circumstances, no."

"You're great, sweet," he said. He put money on the table and got up. "What's the date today?"

"Date? It's October 29."

Andrew blew her a kiss and hurried out.

On the forecourt, two men were unloading a refrigerator from a truck, while Mrs. Maynard was telling them how to do it. Already unloaded were stove, dishwasher, and sink unit.

"Good afternoon, ma'am," Andrew said. "Anyone at home?"

Mrs. Maynard broke off her instructions long enough to say a bleak "Everyone."

"Most kind," Andrew murmured. He went on and into the kitchen, where a plumber was at work with a blowtorch. In the city, Andrew reflected, having a plumber call was slightly easier than getting the Governor-General to stop by for a drink.

Voices were coming from the living room. Andrew announced his approach with a cough, which brought a reply of "Come in, Mr. Bailey. Saw you drive up. This argument needs an interruption."

The speaker, Andrew saw, was Jack Scott. He stood with his back to the electric fire. His brother was sprawled in an armchair, features sulky, hands toying with a pipe.

Andrew asked, "Want me to play referee?"

Harry Scott said, "This is serious. We've all been taking this thing far too lightly."

Jack explained, "Harry wants to send Elaine to a nursing home, for rest and care. I say it's not necessary."

Andrew: "What does Mrs. Scott say?"

"She hasn't been consulted. Yet."

"And what brought this on so suddenly?"

Harry said, "Elaine had another damn trance an hour ago."

"The writing?"

"Didn't do any," Harry said curtly, dismissingly. "She was in the bath. *That's* the point. Never mind the bloody writing. She had a trance in her bath. God's sake, she could've drowned."

"I told him," Jack said, "that trances are like walking in your sleep. You somehow don't let yourself come to harm. Would you agree with that?"

Andrew said, "One hundred per cent. It's an established medical and scientific fact."

"There you are, Harry. What did I say?"

"I don't give a damn for your scientific facts. My wife's human, not a machine. She could hurt herself. Or worse."

Andrew began to talk earnestly. He had a dreary vision of his investigation being cancelled. After restating the safety of the trance state, he said:

"And the increase in frequency shows that a climax is nearing. Then there'll most likely be no more of it. No way is your wife going to spend most of her time in trances."

Jack Scott added, "Certainly not. See reason, Harry."

His brother, still sulky, slapped the pipe onto the table beside him and pushed himself up. "Let's leave it for now," he said. "But don't think I'm forgetting the idea." He went down a ramp in a corner of the room and through a door.

Andrew made no attempt to hide his exhalation of relief.

Jack Scott gave a short laugh. "This case means a lot to you research people, right?"

"It's the best we've had for a long time."

"I'll do my best with Harry."

"I'd appreciate that."

"But I hope Moina O'Neal starts telling about her sovereigns pretty soon. That, maybe, will be the climax."

"You just never know," Andrew said.

Ten minutes later he left and drove to the old homestead. Inside, unsettled, he prowled around. He would have liked to stay on at the Scott home but hadn't been able to think of a way to draw out the conversation, and there was always the danger of his becoming a nuisance or a bore to the family.

Andrew went into the sewing room and began to go over all the writings produced by Elaine. He read carefully and became more restless.

The telephone rang. Andrew went into the parlour to answer. Lifting the receiver, he heard Harry Scott say, as if continuing a conversation, "And another thing, that nightdress and chair and lamp, they haven't been explained yet."

"I can only tell you what I told Mrs. Scott yesterday," Andrew said. "Which is, I don't know."

"All right. What about the lie-detector test?"

Obviously, Andrew thought, his host was turning neurotic about the investigation. "The test, Mr. Scott," he said, "came out in your wife's favour. It reminded me of a similar affair a couple of years ago." He went on to invent a case in which all turned out sunnily well in the end.

Harry Scott's manner was less churlish by the time the call ended. Lowering the receiver, Andrew stared for a while at the portrait of Moina O'Neal. He got his topcoat and went out.

Walking briskly, he soon reached the houses. Around at

the front he saw that, although there was now another service truck present, three of the Scott vehicles were gone from the shared garage. From the kitchen being refitted came Mrs. Maynard's voice. She was explaining fuses to the electrician.

After a dozen slow turns around the forecourt, Andrew went onto the tarmac lane. He started to jog, making the most of this outing on foot, as well as easing his need for action.

He came to the gatehouse, hesitated, went to the door. There was no answer to his knock, though he could hear a radio playing faintly. He knocked again, loud and long. There was still no answer.

Andrew shuddered. He told himself it was the cold, starting to bite now that he had ended the jog.

A third rapping bringing no response, Andrew turned the handle and tried the door. It was unlocked. He went inside, calling, "Hi, Jim!" He heard only the radio.

The living room was empty. Andrew switched off the music and looked into the bedroom. Also empty. The bathroom likewise. But now he could hear another sound. A bubbling. He went into the kitchen.

On the stove a pan was boiling. Andrew lifted the lid. Out with the billows of steam came a smell of burning. Turning off the heat, he went out the back door, which was also unlocked. The vegetable garden was deserted.

Andrew cupped both hands to his mouth and called the old man's name. He called four times, turning to the compass points. His voice faded away, leaving the scene more silent than before.

Andrew circled the house and went quickly over to the dirt road. He was taken now by a feeling of urgency. Along the road there was no sign of life in either direction. A leaf came floating down from a nearby bare tree.

In spite of the urgency Andrew told himself there was no real cause for alarm. He went back into the house. In the kitchen he looked again into the pan. Steam gone now, he could see that it held potatoes. He touched one with a matchstick and it disintegrated. The pan bottom was dry.

In the living room Andrew lifted the telephone receiver and dialled the Scott house. In a moment Mrs. Maynard answered. "Bailey here," Andrew said. "Do you know where Jim Webber is?"

"Me? Why should I know where he is?"

Having no answer to that, Andrew asked, "Is he in the habit of wandering off and leaving his house untended?"

"I know nothing about his habits, thank you."

He explained the situation, ending, "He's an old man. He could be lying sick somewhere."

"Well, I can't leave," the housekeeper said. "There's no one else here and I got to keep an eye on these men."

As Andrew disconnected, the card table caught his attention. He stepped across and looked down. The deck was fanned out, and in front of it lay one card, face up. It looked as though Jim Webber had been halfway through a trick.

Andrew went back outside. About to cross the road and go into the trees, he paused on noticing, some fifty feet away, in the roadside depression, something that looked like a bundle of old clothes.

Andrew started walking in that direction. The next second he was running.

The old man was lying face down. Whispering his name, Andrew gently turned him over. There were dirt and blood on his face. His eyes were closed. A pulse was beating on the side of the thin neck.

Bending close, Andrew saw that the blood had come from the nose. He thought Jim must have done that in falling; he

could have tripped or fainted. But he was breathing in a
strange manner, interchanging long breaths with short.

Andrew carefully ran his hands down the thin body. At
one side, his hand met wetness. It was more blood, and still
seeping. This, Andrew knew, was no fall or faint.

Jim Webber groaned. His eyelids flickered. His lips
moved.

Andrew bent lower, whispering, "It's me—Andrew Bailey.
Can you tell me what's wrong, Jim? Can you hear me?"

The old man went still again, but that pulse was still at
work.

Andrew knelt upright. He darted glances all around at the
emptiness. It made him feel helpless. He didn't know what
to do: run back and get a car; telephone for help; set off
walking with Jim in his arms. It was speed that mattered.

Andrew finally decided. He took a chance on the last
choice, and on the fact that he might be doing the wrong
thing in moving the injured man.

Andrew told himself he was being guided by haste, not by
the feeling that it would be wrong to leave Jim Webber
alone, even for ten minutes.

It was like lifting a child. Andrew had no trouble in getting to his feet. Taking long strides—for the most speed with
the least jolting—he set off for the gateway.

In the distance there was a humming sound. It swiftly
grew to a drone, became recognisable as that of a motor.
Andrew stopped walking when the car came into view.

He thought at first that the driver was a man but then saw
it was a woman—Rennie Bates. She brought the car to a fast,
sliding stop, raising a cloud of dust. She jumped out, asking,
"What's wrong? Who's that? Is it old Jim?"

"Quick," Andrew said. "He's badly hurt. Let's go."

Rennie swung around and opened the back door. Andrew

eased himself inside, still holding the limp body. Rennie got back behind the steering wheel. She said:

"We'll be at the doctor's in no time flat."

Andrew shook his head. "He needs more than that. Where's the nearest hospital?"

"Salisbury. Eight miles the other way."

"Good. Let's move."

Rennie reversed at lurching speed, backed into the gateway, went forward again. "What happened, for God's sake?"

Andrew explained briefly. "I found him only a couple of minutes ago."

"Maybe he fell out of a tree. He was hot on bird-nesting."

"All I know is," Andrew said, "he's badly hurt. So get your foot down to the boards."

The car bucked and skittered as it sped along the dirt road. Jim whimpered. His eagle features creased up into a grimace. He made mumbling sounds.

Andrew said quietly, "You're in a car. We're taking you to hospital. You're going to be fine."

Jim Webber went on mumbling. "What?" Andrew whispered, bending his head closer. "What's that?" He straightened as the mumbling faded away.

"What did he say?" Rennie Bates asked. "Did he say anything?"

Andrew said, "No. Keep 'er rolling." He braced himself as the car cornered fast.

Rennie said, "Thank God I came along when I did. I was on my way to see my aunt. She's sick. Gee, I hope poor old Jim's going to be all right."

Andrew hoped so too, but he had severe doubts. Jim Webber's breathing was more erratic than ever and his face was losing his colour. Blood was seeping steadily onto Andrew's leg from the old man's side.

Rennie Bates shot her car onto a hard-top road. Traffic was light. She was able to maintain a good speed and pass any vehicle she came up behind.

Soon they were in the outskirts of a town. The next minute they were screeching to a stop at the front steps of a hospital. Rennie leapt out and opened the back door.

Andrew didn't feel the knocks on his elbow, shoulder, and head while easing the limp form out; he was busy staring at that slow-beating pulse on the scrawny neck.

The confusion of admission was brief. While Jim was hurried off to Emergency, Rennie answered staff questions. She stayed on at the desk to try and reach the Scott family by telephone—the old man, she said, had no relatives.

Andrew went to a waiting room, where he paced and smoked. His worry stayed at the same level. His anger smouldered.

A doctor came into the room briskly. About forty, he was prematurely white and had an exhausted-looking face. He introduced himself as Edward Kahn. Andrew explained again how he had found Jim Webber.

"Even without knowing location," the doctor said, "I would've thought he'd been hit by a car."

"Is that the way the damage looks?"

"Yes. Hit-and-run's a rotten thing."

"Is he bad?" Andrew asked.

"The external damage could be worse. The big problem is internal bleeding. That and his age."

"I hope I didn't make a mistake in moving him."

"None. Don't give it another thought."

"And tell me, Dr. Kahn, what's the prognosis?"

The doctor shrugged tiredly. "At this moment I have no idea."

Alone again, Andrew kicked a chair for relief and lit another cigarette. He tried sitting but found that it made his nerves dance. The blood on his trousers dried.

Rennie Bates looked into the room to say that Mrs. Scott was on her way and that the golf club was sending someone out onto the course to find Jack. She was still trying to contact Harry.

Andrew stood the confining room for another five minutes, then he left the building. Pacing by the front steps, he pictured a car racing noisily and dustily on a long, straight, quiet road.

When the grey Cadillac glided up he went over to it and opened the driver's door. Elaine Scott looked up at him. Her face held more animation than he had ever seen there before. She asked, "How is he?"

"Not good."

"Is it his heart?"

Andrew told what he knew. Already the story was taking on the glibness of repetition.

Elaine Scott asked, "Was he conscious when you found him?"

"No. Well, barely. He got a few words out."

"But not enough to explain?"

"I'll have to work on what he said. See if it makes sense."

The woman got out of the car. "Hit-and-run," she said musingly. "That doesn't seem possible. On a clear road. In daylight."

"It doesn't," Andrew said. "Does it?"

They went inside and into the waiting room. Rennie Bates was there. She told them that Jack was picking up Harry at the farm and they were coming over together.

Mrs. Scott said, "The police will have to be told."

Rennie: "The hospital already did that, as a matter of form. I guess we'll be seeing Sergeant Stamford soon.

They'll pass this on to the Provincial guys, and this happened in Tom Stamford's territory."

Elaine sat down. Andrew could sense that she was withdrawing. He was about to speak to her, bring her back, when the door opened. The doctor came in. He glanced at each of the three people and then began to shake his head.

Half an hour later Andrew was sitting beside Elaine Scott as she drove her Cadillac. The Scott brothers and Rennie Bates were at the hospital seeing to formalities, including the funeral.

Following the Cadillac in a patrol car was Sergeant Thomas Stamford of the Provincial Police's Hamlyn Creek office. He and Andrew had arranged to meet at the gatehouse.

Andrew was slumped low in the seat. His eyes and mouth were hard. He ached with resentment. His investigation had stopped being mainly on behalf of the Ontario Society for Psychical Research; now it was personal.

"He was a decent man," Elaine Scott said. It was the first time either of them had spoken since leaving the hospital.

Andrew roused himself. "Yes."

"It's hard to believe he's dead."

"I'm still digesting that fact," Andrew said. "It would be easier if he hadn't been such a lively old stick."

"That liveliness. He used to knock himself out acting it. He hated to be thought old."

Andrew said, "It's times like this that I envy my assistant her belief in the afterlife."

Elaine Scott looked at him. She asked, "Has she ever made contact with the dead?"

"She claims so."

The woman quickly turned her attention back to the road as a horn blast came from behind. The patrol car drew level,

then went past and hid in its own trail of dust. When that
had gone, Andrew saw that they were on the home stretch.

Fifty feet this side of the gateway, Tom Stamford came to
a gradual halt while arm-signalling to the following car to
do the same. He got out and walked back.

Sergeant Stamford was a tall man in the mid-thirties,
smart in his uniform. His thin face was pale and freckled,
his blond hair was cut so short that from a distance he
looked bald. He had keen blue eyes.

At the driver's window he said, "Could you hold on here,
Elaine, till Mr. Bailey and I take a look at this stretch of
road?"

"Of course, Tom."

"Not," he added to Andrew as they walked ahead together, "that I expect to find anything in the way of marks.
But I have to go through the motions."

"I know how it is, Sergeant."

At the hospital, the policeman's brusque manner had
eased when Andrew mentioned that he himself had once
been a police officer. It could not, he felt, hurt.

After being shown where Jim Webber had been found,
Stamford examined the road thirty feet in each direction
from there. Coming back, he said:

"A body can fly an awful long way, as you know."

Andrew told him, "I don't know, actually. I never did
traffic detail. It's a mystery to me."

"Well, I'll give you this much. On dirt it's mostly a waste
of time, looking. Now if we had a nice damp hard-top, or if
the driver had been kind enough to lose a hubcap . . ."

"Sure," Andrew said. "So what's the routine?"

"Impact damage on the car. The Highway guys are keeping a lookout. I'll check this area, vehicles and people."

"Sergeant, you don't sound too hopeful."

The officer shook his head. "Thing is, there doesn't have

to be damage—and there's no broken glass around. With a big man, maybe. That old Jim, he probably weighed in at a hundred pounds soaking wet."

"Could you tell from marks on the body which way the vehicle had been travelling?"

"Not in this case. Jim wasn't headed any place. He could only have been standing around out here."

Andrew offered cigarettes. Tom Stamford declined and signalled to the Cadillac. It came forward. Elaine Scott waved as she drove onto the tarmac lane.

Andrew blew out smoke. He asked, "So what could've happened?"

"My hunch is that some kid of minus sixteen took the truck out for a fast whip around while his dad was safely in the fields."

"And the hit?"

"Kid sees pedestrian, zooms close to give him a scare, misjudges distance, bang, and good-bye."

"In a case like that," Andrew said, "I can see the reason for the run. Otherwise no."

"Oh, sure. Lots of reasons for failing to stop. The insurance just lapsed, or the driver's licence. The car's hot. The driver's up to something illegal, or in any case can't afford to get involved with the law. It's a businessman or tourist who can't handle the delay. It's a recent immigrant who thinks he'll be put against a wall and shot. It's someone who's hiding a disability that would get his licence revoked. I could go on."

Andrew said, "It gets worse and worse."

"Well, as I told you before, there's people, the locals, even without impact damage. I'm talking about alibi."

"I don't have one."

"Neither do I," the policeman said. "Harry was on the farm someplace, Elaine was in the hairdresser's, Jack was on the golf course, and young Rennie was closing up the office to sneak a visit to her aunt."

Andrew gave a wry grin. "You don't leave anyone out, do you?"

"Nope. And there's service people at the Scotts'. Also, I'll be checking out regular users of this road. But frankly, I think I'm onto a loser."

"The prospect isn't too bright," Andrew agreed. "What about the inquest?"

"Tomorrow, I hope. Hold yourself available, as we say in the trade."

"I'll be around," Andrew said, and said it in so firm a way that the policeman looked at him curiously.

Tom Stamford nodded. "Sure. There's your own investigation. This writing thing of Elaine's. It's the number one topic of the moment. Hot on the trail?"

As they walked to the patrol car, Andrew touched on various facets of the case. When they were driving off, he ended, "That Moina O'Neal must've been quite a gal."

"Sure," Stamford said. "But back to old Jim. Did you check inside the house?"

"Just looked inside and saw he wasn't there."

"You didn't know him well, of course."

"Hardly at all."

Tom Stamford drove along the tarmac lane to the forecourt, which he began to by-pass. Andrew said, "This'll do for me. I can walk from here."

"I guess you could," the officer said, winking. "But I'd like to check your car out."

"Sergeant, you'll make chief inspector yet."

"Glad you approve." He brought the car to a halt by the stoop. Andrew could hear the telephone ringing inside. Opening the door, he said, "There's my car. Help yourself. See you." He hurried into the house.

The caller was John Bright. He said, "Been trying to get you for an hour, Chief."

"Things have been happening. I'll fill you in on that in a minute. What happened in the country?"

"Well, I blocked the safety valve, half filled it with water and put her on the fire. And wow. Good job I was standing well back from that baby."

"A blast?"

"I'll say. If a pressure cooker had exploded in that kitchen, it would've blown the back wall out."

It had taken Ann an hour to win the freedom of the morgue. The first half of that time she spent traipsing from one office or person to another in the vast building off Bloor Street in downtown Toronto. Everybody seemed to have a different opinion on who exactly was in charge of the files and reference section; everybody, that is, who was aware of its existence.

Once Ann had found the right man, who looked like the janitor, it developed that he was so low on the job scale that he naturally had to overcompensate.

He was officious, despotic, superior. It took a lot of flattering persuasion before Ann was allowed alone into the sprawling basement that smelt of used air and socks.

It was a maze of shelves, empty beer bottles and redundant furniture, all lit by naked, low-watt bulbs. The gloom helped soothe Ann back to normal from her fury with the morgue's guardian.

She had no trouble finding the shelf she wanted. Using both hands, she drew out a large, thick volume of bound newspapers, the previous year's November editions.

Carrying it to a table, she paused at hearing a sound from behind her. She turned. There was nothing to be seen among the banks of shelves that stood at various angles.

Ann sat down and opened the volume to the first newspaper. The front page held nothing relating to her search. That she came across on page three. It was a disappointingly small item, stating briefly that a Mrs. Cicelia Scott had been shot and killed on a roadside near Hamlyn Creek, Ont. Police were investigating.

Ann turned to the next day's edition, where, though still on the third page, the story had grown and become the White Witch Murder. What details were given Ann knew already. This pertained in editions covering the following two days.

Ann looked around at a noise. A man came backing into view from around a bank of shelves, his arms full of books. He turned, saw Ann, and stopped. He was big and handsome and fair.

"Hi," he said. "Are you our new cookery genius?"

Ann shook her head. "I know your face. Don't tell me. I'll get it in a minute."

The man crashed the books onto the table, looked at his watch and started counting backward from sixty.

Ann laughed and held up a hand. "I give in."

"Haig Wilson," the man said. "You've probably seen my pic on the sports page."

"Yes, and I've heard about you from Andrew."

"Andrew?"

"Andrew Bailey. Ontario Society for Psychical Research. I'm Ann Goodwin, his assistant."

The reporter had been nodding. He said, "And I've heard of you, from Elaine Scott. She says you're smart and pretty."

"Well, isn't that nice of her."

They began to talk of the automatic writing. Haig Wilson half sat on the table and swung one leg. Ann thought him the most magnetically masculine man she had ever met, as well as one of the handsomest. His manner, however, seemed natural, without vanity, though possibly he did show his perfect teeth more often than necessary.

Ann said, "I'm glad none of your colleagues have had wind of these trances. It was good of you not to tell them."

The sports writer looked surprised. "The Scotts are my friends."

"I like that."

"In any case, when they told me, they knew it wouldn't go any further."

"But everyone in that area's heard about it."

"As Jack said, it's useless trying to keep anything a secret around the Creek."

"So it's bound to be picked up by a newshound sooner or later."

"Maybe it won't go on long enough," Haig Wilson said. "And talking of news, what're you researching?"

Hoping she was doing the right thing, Ann said, "That terrible affair last year with Cissy Scott." She added, "I won't tell Andrew about being here, doing this. I get curious about these things, which he thinks foolish of me."

"Your secret is in a grave."

"Thanks." Feeling slightly nervous, she reached in her pocketbook for cigarettes.

Haig Wilson said, "Well, I'll save you a reading chore. I know all the details. Professional instinct."

"Great. To begin with, you could tell me why the Scott girls didn't drive right up to the farm."

"The service lane. Usually at this time of year—we've been lucky so far—the rain or snow, plus frost, has the lanes a squelchy mess. Just about okay for trucks."

"So they planned to walk to all the farms?"

Haig Wilson nodded. He pointed at the cigarette Ann was lighting. "I could help you give up those things, if you sincerely wanted to."

"I'd feel a prig if I didn't have at least one vice," Ann said. "But go on. The trial. What happened?"

"Very little. It lasted about seven minutes. The prosecution accepted the psychiatric report on Benny Kaiser that he was mentally unfit to plead. He was sentenced to be detained during Her Majesty's pleasure, which is a nice way of saying forever."

"How old is he?"

"Nineteen, twenty. Lived with an old grandfather, who's died since. Benny confessed at first to both the killing and previous molesting charges, then later claimed he was innocent. But he'd been caught at the Romeo game. He chased a woman tourist who'd had a flat on a back road. A farmer came along—and there you go."

Ann drew thoughtfully on her cigarette. "Maybe the gun went off accidentally."

The reporter shook his head. "That wouldn't have caused much damage. Jack made the first shell in the gun a blank. Cissy had gotten it from the theatre. That was fired and then two more. I guess the kid panicked."

"And that was the end of it all?"

"Not quite. There was the formality of charging Harry with illegal importation and possession of a handgun. He'd bought the revolver on a trip to the States. Thousands do it. Harry was fined a nominal hundred bucks, plus confiscation, of course."

Ann closed the volume of newspapers, causing a baby storm of dust. "What makes the case worse is that it's so unglamorous. A beautiful, vivacious woman killed for no good reason. How awful. How stupid."

"There're much juicier cases I could tell you the inside stories of," Haig Wilson said, giving his warmest smile yet. "If you're a murder fan. For instance, that triple slaying in Windsor this spring."

It was half an hour before Ann was able to get away, her mind full of gore and hatchets and weird developments. Leaving the building, she went to a drugstore and telephoned the home of Moina O'Neal. Andrew answered.

He listened to Ann's report and then told about his own day. Ann didn't know if it was the effect of Haig Wilson's storytelling, but the news about Jim Webber made her shudder violently.

"God," she said. "That's appalling. And how dreadful for you."

"Worse for old Jim."

"Andrew, your voice sounds . . ."

But he was moving on. After telling of John Bright's test with the cooker, he said:

"Since then, nothing until a few minutes ago. Mrs. Maynard came in with an envelope. It's Elaine's latest writing, straight from her hand. That's her second trance today."

I can't help it if I feel the growth of hate. It seems beyond my control. The old battle between logic and emotion. I'm ashamed of myself but can't do anything about it. I suppose I would feel easier if I had a definite goal for the hatred. It's split like a greenstick fracture. All jagged. Dangerous. The division is because of more than one being involved. Involved and committed. It was better when there was doubt, but I didn't know it. Before that, a fool's paradise. Maybe I was born stupid. I've always acted otherwise, though. Like a sick dog trying to be frisky. And now I'm the brokenhearted clown in the song. The show must go on. It's God-awful to be civilised. Pity the Anglo-Saxon. The Latins are much better at it. But I have to hold on. I mustn't get a persecution complex. I mustn't think of it as a conspiracy. That's an easy trap to get caught by, like self-pity.

I've even started to think the weather's against me. It rained throughout the day and, all things being equal, it will freeze throughout the night. Rain is such a downer. I said that to her without thinking—funny how you can forget your part—and she gave me an old-fashioned look. I nearly, very nearly, brought the whole thing out. Let it splurge from me like vomit. That I might actually do so shatters me. I left quickly. But I do need to tell. Need a wailing wall, mother confessor, shoulder of comfort. In a book I once read the heroine tells her terrible secret to a friend who's stone deaf. Feels better for it. That's what I could do with. Maybe I'll try a mirror. But that'll only show me I'm not as young as I used to be. Which is childish. That isn't what's at issue. I only torture myself more by spiking myself on these minor prongs. Maybe I do it to avoid the other thing. Not easy to face it. But it still could be my imagination. I shouldn't have played the game of enquiry, eliminating one possibility after another. After going through fear, and worry, and perverse hope, and rage, I came to what I thought was the answer: hate. But no, that's the other. This has nothing to do with emotion. It's not mine. And the atmosphere is death.

SIX

The children had been sent home at recess. Parts of words and sums remained around the edges of the hurriedly cleaned blackboard, and motes of chalk dust still hovered in the streams of pale sunshine.

Relinquishing her place at the large desk to the coroner, a feed dealer, the schoolteacher sat nearby in her new role as clerk of the court. Behind her sat the jury, six men whose expressions ranged from petulance to mild interest.

In the pupils' desks were Andrew, Sergeant Stamford, Rennie Bates, the Scott brothers and Elaine Scott, plus Dr. Kahn, a pathologist from the same hospital, and a dozen of the curious.

The coroner, an older man with age spots like flung paint, nodded at the policeman. Tom Stamford unwound himself from the cramped seating. Pink-faced, he said:

"Oyez, oyez, oyez. Hear ye that this inquest into the death of James Webber is now in session, Ainsworth Carmondy, Justice of the Peace, presiding. God save the Queen." He sat again.

The feed dealer said, "Would Mr. Andrew Bailey take the stand, please."

Andrew got up and went forward. The stand, as indicated by a nod from the coroner, was an area of floor space by a corner of the desk. With hands clasped behind and feet spread, Andrew began to tell of the incidents of yesterday.

He needed no prompting. Nor did he lose the thread of

his story. For one thing, he was used to giving evidence; for another, this was his seventh or eighth recounting of the affair. He had it neat.

As he talked, he looked around the gathering, from the coroner, to the jury, to the involved, to the curious.

Everyone was attentive, in some degree, with the single exception of Elaine Scott. Sitting between her husband and brother-in-law, she was gazing at different sections of the ceiling. Occasionally she closed her eyes for short periods, almost like protracted blinks. She was paler than usual.

"I examined Mr. Webber," Andrew said. "He was alive but bleeding. He was obviously badly hurt."

The coroner looked at the tip of his pen. "You have medical experience, Mr. Bailey?"

"No, sir. It was, admittedly, a layman's assessment."

"Thank you. Please continue."

Andrew noted that Elaine was now staring at the blackboard. Her eyes slowly closed, slowly opened. Andrew felt alarm at the possibility of her going into a trance here: a writing opportunity wasted. He began to speak faster.

"Wait, please," the schoolteacher said. "Let me get that last bit down."

Tense, Andrew waited. Elaine Scott closed her eyes. This time she kept them closed. Andrew wondered what her right hand was doing.

The teacher said, "Go on, please."

"That's about all. I got Mr. Webber into Miss Bates's car and we drove him to the hospital."

The coroner asked, "He was still unconscious?"

"Mostly, yes."

"What does mostly mean, Mr. Bailey?"

"He was unconscious in degrees from light to deep," Andrew said. "He moaned and mumbled."

"He didn't form any words?"

"He did not."

Elaine Scott opened her eyes. Languidly she leaned sideways, toward her husband. Her lips moved. Harry Scott nodded. Elaine began to get up.

The coroner looked around. "Does anyone have a question for this witness?"

To Andrew's annoyance, one of the jurymen lifted a hand. He said, "I have."

"Go ahead."

The man asked, "Did the witness see anything of an unusual nature when he was looking in the house?"

Watching Elaine Scott, who was moving to a door at the back of the room, Andrew said, "No, sir. Nothing. Everything appeared to be quite normal."

"Oh," the juryman said, as Elaine left the schoolroom. "Well, I guess that's all."

Again the coroner asked for questions. There were none. He said, "Witness may stand down. Thank you."

Andrew moved away. He went past the front seats, past where the curious were sitting, and waited by an empty place. When the feed dealer said, "Dr. Edward Kahn, please," Andrew went on and slipped out quietly.

As he came onto the street, the Cadillac was drawing away. He hurried to his own car, got in and started the motor. Not until the big grey limousine had turned a corner did he pull out to follow.

Andrew, whose skill at car-tailing was another legacy from his police days, continued this pattern of seek and hide until out of the village. In country the hide periods became longer. But he had no worry about losing his quarry: the Cadillac's passage was clearly marked by its trail of dust.

Andrew rolled up his window and turned the heater higher. It had become colder. The faint sun had gone. The midday sky was as dull as evening.

The trip was short. The dust faded by a church that stood alone at a crossroads. Andrew went as close as he dared before stopping. He got out. For a better view he stood on the hood of the car.

In a moment he could pick out Elaine Scott. She was in the cemetery beside the church, standing still, her head lowered. Andrew wished he had binoculars.

The cold breeze made his eyes water. The moisture increased. After wiping it away on a handkerchief he looked back at the cemetery. Elaine had gone. Next he saw the Cadillac moving. It was coming this way.

Quickly Andrew jumped down and got back inside. He did a rapid back and fill, shot the car forward. Now he would have to tail by leading. He had done that before as well.

Andrew went straight on at the first junction. After a short stretch he slowed to lower his dust marker. The top of the big car came into sight. He speeded up again. This he did twice more, until it became fairly evident where Elaine Scott was heading.

His last reduction was beyond the gatehouse. Dying dust was there, but not the grey limousine. Andrew reversed and also went onto the tarmac lane. On nearing the forecourt, however, he saw that the carport held only the two blue trucks. He steered around behind the houses.

After a hundred yards he stopped. He got out, made no sound in closing the door and set off at a brisk walk. Soon the old homestead came into view. Near it was parked the Cadillac, empty.

Andrew ran the rest of the way.

He stepped softly onto the stoop, as softly eased open the door. At that point he halted. He could hear a voice. It was Elaine Scott's.

"It's the pressure, you see," she was saying. Her voice was

so low that Andrew had to strain to hear. She was in the parlour. "It's heavy. Like a weight."

A pause, and, "I wish you could talk to me, the way you used to. It was such a comfort. I remember it well. If only I could go back to that."

After another pause Elaine went on, her tone plaintive, "Can't you hear me, Gran? Are you nowhere at all? Can't you give me some kind of sign?"

There was no more talking. Andrew, breathing shallowly, heard faint sounds of movement. When these also ended, the silence was total inside.

Andrew waited five minutes. About to enter, he held back as the telephone shrilled. The call signal went on. It rang time after time, with no sound from inside to indicate that it was going to be answered. That was good enough for Andrew.

He went in. He didn't trouble too greatly to hide his presence. The parlour was empty. Elaine Scott he found in the sewing room, and, as he had guessed, she was in a trance.

She sat at the open writing desk. Her right hand held a pen, her left kept firm a piece of paper—the blank side of an old letter. She was writing; writing, it seemed, with more determination than previously.

The telephone stopped ringing.

Andrew moved to the woman's side. He looked over her shoulder at the writing. He noted the now familiar urgency in the cryptic style and the short sentences.

Elaine came to the bottom of the page. She turned over to the used side, hesitated. Andrew swiftly found a piece of clean paper and pushed it into position. Elaine started writing again.

Andrew picked up the old letter and began deciphering. As soon as he had a sentence or phrase or paragraph clear, he read it over aloud if he felt it had significance. There were not many like that. The rest were doubtful or obscure. Andrew read out:

"This thing about death. It's definite now. But I still don't understand it. I hope I'm not getting sick ideas in a totally new direction.

"The deceit is vile. Was it yesterday I said that about vile and evil having the same letters? I think he went pale. But he doesn't guess what I know. That's positive.

"I must keep pain out of my head. This morning when I began to think that way I got busy with the dishwasher and—"

"Mrs. Scott! Are you all right?"
Andrew swung around.
Into the room bustled Mrs. Maynard. Her hair was mussed, her topcoat unbuttoned, her face anxious. She went straight past, toward her employer, and again called her name.

"Quiet," Andrew snapped. Then he swore as the housekeeper began to shake Elaine Scott's arm.

Andrew strode forward. It was too late. The trance had been interrupted. Elaine let the pen fall and lifted both hands to her cheeks. She whimpered.

Heavily, Andrew asked, "Just what the hell do you think you're doing, Mrs. Maynard?"

The stout woman, hotly defensive, said, "I saw her go by the house. I called here and there was no answer. So I came. She's not well. That's the second time today this's happened."

"What?"
"This trance, as you call it."
Andrew perked. "When was the other?"
"After breakfast," Mrs. Maynard said, settling. "Mrs.

Scott was filling out a check for my wages, and she suddenly
started to write all over it."

Andrew managed to produce a friendly smile. "And what
did you do with the check, ma'am?"

"Do with it? Why, I burned it, of course. They never
would've cashed it at the bank."

Andrew sighed. He said, "No, probably not."

The housekeeper bent solicitously over Elaine Scott, asking, "How d'you feel, dear?" Next, abruptly, she straightened to ask in a sharp voice:

"What was that you were saying as I came in? Something
about a dishwasher?"

"That's right."

"Well, there were no dishwashing machines in Moina
O'Neal's day, let me tell you."

Nodding, Andrew leaned forward and picked up the
unfinished page. "That's true," he said. "The writing wasn't
referring to a machine but to a person. Someone in the
kitchen at a party."

"Oh," Mrs. Maynard said, slowly and bleakly.

"I hope it's going to be all right," Maude Herman said.

Ann shook her head impatiently. "I do wish you'd stop
this worrying. Everything's fine."

"That's what you say."

"I mean it, Maude. Would I lie to you?"

The woman thought that one over. She said, "Certainly."

"Gee, thanks."

They were in Ann's car, which was rattling its way along
a back road. Ann being nervous, her driving was erratic. She
didn't like the thought of what Andrew would say when he
found out about the project—unless, of course, it was successful.

Ann turned the Volkswagen at a crossroads. She said, "We're nearly there."

"Oh dear," Mrs. Herman said. She was a matron of early middle age, with an uncared-for appearance and clothes that had long passed out of fashion. Her spectacles needed polishing. She operated, with her husband, a coffee shop in a Toronto suburb. She was also the best-known spiritualist medium in Ontario.

With a frown she asked, "You're quite sure Andrew knows all about this? And the police?"

"Absolutely," Ann lied glibly. "Otherwise, how would I know how to get in the place?" She knew because Andrew had mentioned Jim Webber's habit of keeping a key under the doormat. "Not a thing to worry about."

"Ann, I never saw you smoke so much."

"That's excitement," Ann said, not wholly lying. "The old man died within the last twenty-four hours. And suddenly, unexpectedly. It looks good."

Maude Herman's pleasant face became pretty as she smiled. "You know, you have far more faith in me than I have."

"I discovered you, Maude. Both Andrew and John Bright are baffled at your results."

"So am I."

Not unusual among non-professional sensitives, Maude Herman had no explanation for what seemed a supranormal gift. She didn't know why she had dreams that came true, or could tell a stranger facts about his past, or was able to get information from an inanimate object. This last, telekinesis, was her forte.

Where the practising medium talked of wave lengths and ether, metagnomy and auras, the more powerful amateur spoke of headaches, nausea, and stomach cramps, and on the whole would have preferred to be ungifted. It was a difficult situation, being nervous of oneself.

Ann saw the gatehouse up ahead. "There it is," she said, beginning to slow. "I think we'll park here."

"What for?"

"Well, so we won't disturb any vibrations." She was aware of how absurd that sounded, but it would have to do.

Mrs. Herman said, "Me, I'd park right in front."

And let everyone know where we are, Ann thought, if we don't get through before they come back from the inquest.

She stopped the car and got out. "Come on." During the short walk to the house she resisted the urge to look at her watch or get out another cigarette. The medium hadn't to be flurried, if she was to do her best work.

Without trouble Ann found the key and opened the front door. She led the way inside. In a small, neat living room she asked, "How do you want to do this, Maude?"

Mrs. Herman shrugged, looking around uncertainly. "The same as always, I guess. Wait and see what happens."

"Cards," Ann said. "Jim Webber played cribbage a lot. Here. Sit here, Maude."

The medium sat in a high-backed chair facing a table on which were scoreboard and a neatly stacked deck of cards. These she touched lightly at first, her finger ends trembling. Next she handled the deck and moved the peg along the board.

Ann stood by the wall and watched with care. She tried not to be envious.

Mrs. Herman appeared dissatisfied with the objects on the table. Clasping the arms of the chair, she leaned her head back. She relaxed. She let her eyelids droop. She breathed deeply.

Several minutes passed. Ann looked fretfully at her watch.

She started when Maude Herman spoke, even though it was only to utter a single, mundane word. The woman said:

"Potatoes."

"What?" Ann gasped, and could have kicked herself for interrupting.

Mrs. Herman sat forward, eyes open. She asked, "What was that I said? Sounded like potatoes."

Ann nodded. "Yes. But never mind. Go back. Go back to where you were."

"Wherever that may be."

"Just relax."

"I wonder what was the last thing he touched?"

"I don't know," Ann said. "I don't suppose anyone knows. Go back, Maude."

The sensitive eased down and lowered her eyelids. As before, she was clasping the arms of the chair.

Ann tensed on hearing a distant whine. She knew it was a vehicle approaching. The sound grew, came level, went past, faded. Ann stayed tense.

Mrs. Herman began to hum deep in her throat. Then she spoke, whispering, "Sure," and "Be right out." She put one hand on the table and felt around until she came to the deck of cards, which she held.

She murmured, "Anything for a friend."

Ann jerked her head around. There had been a noise, here in the house. It had come from beyond an interior door. It led, Ann thought, to the kitchen.

"No problem," Mrs. Herman whispered. "No sweat."

Ann was staring at the door. The noise had been repeated. It was like that made by someone moving about, but stealthily. Ann felt her scalp begin to tingle.

Holding the pack of cards in both hands, Maude Herman whispered, "No, I'm not tired. Be right there."

Ann clenched her fists. The sounds were still going on.

They were closer now to the door, which shuddered. Then it flew open.

Ann let out a cry. Maude Herman sat bolt upright. They both stared at the man in the doorway. Or rather, they stared at the gun in his hand, while noting secondarily that he wore a uniform.

The man said, "Now just who might you folks be?"

Ann began on a stammered explanation. She introduced herself and her friend. She apologised for entering the house without official permission, but claimed that Mr. Bailey had said it would be all right, then took that back:

"At least, I think that's what he said. I'm not sure."

The policeman had been slowly putting his gun away. He clipped the flap down, asking, "What were those names again?"

Ann told him. "And you must be Sergeant Stamford. How do you do. Andrew told me about you. How did the inquest go?" She smiled brightly.

"Death by misadventure, caused by a person or persons unknown."

"Well, there you are."

"Also tell me again," Stamford said, "*what* are you ladies doing here?"

Ann repeated her explanation. The officer looked at Mrs. Herman with an expression midway between pique and disbelief. "You were trying to contact the spirit of Jim Webber?"

The sensitive shrugged, and Ann said, "Something like that."

"So did you?"

Maude Herman said, "I don't think I did. I wasn't feeling too peculiar. Only a bit."

Disbelief thrived in the policeman's face. He said, "If

you're a spiritualist medium, ma'am, tell me what I'm going to do today."

Maude Herman smiled. She put down the cards and said, "I don't have the slightest idea."

"I'm not surprised to hear it."

"But I know what you were doing this morning."

"Sure you do. I was at an inquest."

"Before that. You were at a car repair shop."

Tom Stamford blinked. After that he smiled. "Of course. You ladies saw me in the Creek."

Ann and Mrs. Herman protested that they hadn't driven through Hamlyn Creek on their way here. The policeman went on smiling indulgently. At last he said:

"Anyway, ladies, I'm afraid I must ask you to please vacate the premises."

An hour and a half later Andrew, Ann, and Maude Herman were finishing a late lunch in the kitchen of the old homestead. The women had brought the picnic-style fixings with them, and as these were all Andrew's favourites, from dill pickles to corned beef, the ambience had quickly lost its initial chill.

As far as Andrew was concerned, real warmth had come when he heard about what the sensitive had said in the late Jim Webber's house. He had made Ann go over everything a second time.

Now Andrew was telling of the latest writing produced by Elaine Scott. He said, "The urgency's stronger than ever."

Ann nodded. "So is yours. You haven't unwound any since I saw you yesterday."

"Since then I've lost a friend. But apart from that, anything could be happening in the Scott house. Any other writing she does is liable to be destroyed."

Maude Herman said, "Maybe it wouldn't be a bad idea to do what the husband wants—put her in a nursing home. You could arrange to have her watched."

Andrew said, "I've thought of that. But it's here that she has to be."

Ann stirred her coffee. "Why?"

"Because."

"Andrew, I get the feeling that you're keeping a lot back, which is not all that unusual."

"Keeping a lot back from myself, if you know what I mean. Things're still jelling in the grey cells."

"And you haven't come up with an excuse to get yourself firmly in the Scott place?"

Andrew shook his head. The sensitive asked, "But didn't you say the husband was worried about his wife? That even the housekeeper was?"

"That's right."

"Then the answer's simple. Get Ann installed. You tell them she's a nurse, a certified professional, and that she'd be happy to move in."

Andrew and Ann unisoned a low, impressed "Hey."

Maude Herman added, "Ann won't mind lying. She does it all the time."

Andrew got up quickly and went into the parlour. He lifted the telephone receiver and dialled the Scotts. Harry answered. After hearing the reason for the call, he began to hedge: he didn't know, he wasn't sure, he felt that Elaine would . . .

"Mrs. Scott doesn't have to know," Andrew cut in. "About Miss Goodwin being a nurse and staying because of that."

"So how do we explain her stay?"

As Andrew was about to admit that he didn't know, he got an idea. He said, "We say Miss Goodwin wants to stay over tonight but doesn't think it's proper to stay here in this house."

"Yes, Elaine would go for that all right, and the stopover could be explained by the snow, but I still . . ."

"What snow?"

Harry Scott said, "The load we're going to get any time now. The sky's full of it. But as I was saying, I don't know if this is the right thing."

Andrew started to talk at his most persuasive. This time, it was the other man who cut in. He said, "Here's Jack. I'll see what he thinks."

Andrew smiled confidently. He was unsurprised when Harry Scott came back on the line to say, "Well, my brother seems to agree with you, so I guess it's okay."

Andrew made his report in the kitchen. Ann rubbed her hands together. Maude Herman got up: "If it's going to snow, I'd better set off back."

They walked out with her to the Volkswagen. Buttoning her topcoat, Maude asked, "Andrew, what's the name of that tune you were whistling a while back?"

"I? I wasn't whistling."

"Must have been you, Ann. I've got it running through my head."

"Maude, I don't know how to whistle. And I wouldn't if I could because my mother says ladies shouldn't."

"Ah well," the sensitive said. "Maybe it was in my own head all the time. I thought I'd picked it up." She opened the car door. "Hope I'll be all right in this wreck."

Ann asked, "What is the tune that's bugging you?"

"No idea. Goes like this." She hummed.

"I've no idea either," Ann said.

"It's called 'Diamonds Are Forever,'" Andrew told them. He turned away. "'Bye, Maude."

Back in the kitchen, he and Ann tidied up from the meal.

Ann asked, "Sure you're not mad at me for going to the gatehouse?"

"Angry. No." He kissed her on the cheek. "I'm glad you did it."

"Good. But it wasn't a real success, was it? Also, Maude didn't feel a thing here in Moina's house."

"Let's hurry this up."

"I never saw anyone in such a bustle."

"Time's getting short," Andrew said.

"The snow, you mean?"

"Let's go."

They went out, got in the Ford, moved off. Andrew let Ann out at the forecourt, then drove on toward town. His feeling of haste should have slackened, now that he had an assured watchdog in the Scott home, but it hadn't. The early-darkening day was a further prod.

In Hamlyn Creek, Andrew parked on a side street. As he left the car he saw a woman preparing the path to her front door. She was rubbing it with a cake of cattle salt lick.

There were no cars standing in front of the barn theatre. The side door was unlocked, however, and once inside Andrew heard someone humming. With a feeling of déjà vu he went quietly along the passage.

At the half-open door he peered into the auditorium. The hummer was Rennie Bates. She was on the stage dividing a pile of clothes into two smaller piles. Andrew waited.

Ten minutes passed. When Rennie went into the wings, Andrew slipped inside and went on tiptoe to the rear of the hall, where he crouched down behind the seats. Rennie returned and her work went on, as did the humming.

Andrew's legs beginning to stiffen, he lowered himself sideways onto the floor. He realised, with despondency, that the girl could be planning to stay for hours.

But no sooner had he become resigned to that possibility

than she stopped humming and sorting, switched off the one strong light and left. The outer door clicked shut.

Andrew got up. He walked down the centre aisle and climbed onto the stage. To the right in the wings, clearly marked, were the dressing rooms. Utilities were on the left. Andrew headed there, picking his way past clothes, hampers, paint cans, empty bottles, discarded junk-food packages.

In a room designated Storage, he began to look about. There were costumes and props and all a theatre's impedimenta. Andrew searched in drawers and boxes until he found what he wanted.

A corner of the room was set up as an office. Andrew looked in the telephone directory, got a number, dialled it. A voice answered with "Hello. Claud Trubolt speaking."

"Andrew Bailey here, Mr. Trubolt. I was wondering about your next production. When will it be?"

It was a quarter hour before Andrew could stem the verbal flow, get around to the real purpose of his call—which, he mentioned idly, he was making from the O'Neal place.

He asked, "What plays have the group put on over the last couple of years?"

This time the director was brief, limiting himself to names and dates. He sounded amused. He had taken over the directing post only recently.

After chatting for a minute longer, Andrew disconnected. He set off to leave the theatre. However, something on the stage caught his eye and jogged his memory. He returned to the office area and again used both directory and telephone. His call was short, and satisfying.

As Andrew put down the receiver he heard a car horn. He left the storage room and made his way to the inner door. He went along the passage.

From outside came the sound of a cough.

Swinging around, Andrew went back into the auditorium and up onto the stage and into the wings. He stopped. He wasn't sure himself why he was going through these motions of avoidance.

The outer door opened and closed. A male voice, muffled by the passage, called cheerfully, "Rennie! You there, Ren?"

Andrew went deeper into the wings, past doors and clutter, flies and hanging sandbags. In deep gloom he descended steps to ground level. There he found a roughhewn door. He unbolted it and slipped out.

Back at his car Andrew got in and drove out of town. It was seven miles to the golf course. The clubhouse, pseudo Tudor, came into view first. Signs pointed to the parking area, hidden by a belt of trees. On arriving there, Andrew saw only three cars, all unknown to him. He drove away.

Back in town he parked on the main street and went into a hardware store. He was oblivious to what normally would have pleased him: the piquant smell of leather, oil, and rope.

A clerk approached. Andrew asked to speak to the proprietor, was told he was busy for the moment, said he would wait. He made a pretence of browsing.

A sporting calendar caught Andrew's attention. Not its picture, but its date. It reminded him that the next day was Halloween.

Ann, standing by the picture window, turned her head as she glimpsed a movement. It seemed to be in the darkness of the trees in the near distance. But it was actually a few feet away, she saw.

The movement was a snowflake. It had become visible only after leaving its backdrop of grey-white sky. Large and fluffy, it drifted gently forward.

The reason Ann watched the flake until it landed, and then began to look for others, was to occupy her mind, keep tranquil. Her excitement at being here in the Scott house was still high. For two hours she had sat, tried to read a magazine, switched the television on and off. But nothing had happened.

The Scott brothers had left soon after her arrival. The housekeeper had looked in once to ask if she needed anything. And as for Elaine, she had been totally absent, not even deigning to make a gesture of welcome.

"Resting," Harry Scott had said, showing the door of his wife's room. "If you could just give a listen every once in a while?"

"Of course."

"I'd stay home myself, but with snow on the way, we have things to see to."

Ann had done the listening, at intervals of ten minutes to begin with, though the lapses had grown when all seemed well. On the last check she had tried the door, found it unlocked and peeked inside. Elaine Scott was not to be seen, but sounds of splashing had been coming from the bathroom.

Now Ann found another snowflake, and another. There were more. She started to count but a gust of wind blew a horde of the fluffy blobs into view.

The white attack had started in earnest.

"Miss Goodwin?"

Ann turned around. Mrs. Maynard was in the arch that led to kitchen and sleeping quarters. She held a dish towel and a wooden spoon. Looking faintly defiant, she said:

"I wanted to ask you something."

Here it comes, Ann thought. Where was I a probationer and when did I get my nursing degree? "Yes, Mrs. Maynard?"

"It's about your Mr. Bailey," the woman said. "I've just

been listening to a report of the inquest on the radio. And it seems to me something's wrong."

"Wrong with the inquest?"

"With what Mr. Bailey told them. He told them he hadn't been inside Jim Webber's house, only looked in. But he must've gone in because he used the telephone. He called me."

"Oh, really?"

"He wanted to know if I knew where old Jim was."

Not having a suitable comment, Ann nodded. The housekeeper said, "And that's what I wanted to ask you. Should I tell Tom Stamford? It might be important. And I guess it just slipped Mr. Bailey's mind." She no longer looked defiant. Her expression was sleepy with satisfaction.

Ann said coldly, "I'll speak to Mr. Bailey about it. Thank you for bringing the matter to my attention."

Bitch, she thought, turning away, and then forgot the woman, whom she heard leaving, on seeing how greatly the falling snow had increased. The forecourt was almost covered.

Ann thought of foam, next of soap, next of Elaine Scott, who should be through with her bath by now. She had to be.

Ann went quickly to the familiar door. She tapped. Getting no response, she went in. Her haste ebbed as she saw the woman. In a robe, the ends of her blond hair dark with wet, she sat in an armchair beside a radiator, faced the other way.

When Elaine didn't raise her head or look around, Ann's nerves pricked again. She strode forward and knelt down beside the chair. Her presence was not acknowledged.

Through near-closed eyes, Mrs. Scott was gazing at her right hand. On the lap of her robe, it appeared to be making miniature patterns.

Swiftly, her heart tapping, Ann found a pad and pen. These she took to the woman and put carefully into place. With a small sigh, Elaine Scott began to write.

Ann stood back and watched. She held her hands together tightly. For the second time that day, she steeled herself against a feeling of envy.

The writing continued for three pages. After that the hand sagged away and let the pen fall. The pad slipped to the floor. Ann went over, bent, and took off the three pages of writing, which she quickly folded and put into the neckline of her dress.

Elaine Scott drew in a long, slow breath through her nose. At the same time, as though she were a balloon being filled by the air she was taking in, she sat up erect and lifted her head.

She looked at Ann dully, asking, "What's wrong?"

"Nothing, Mrs. Scott. You dozed off."

She moved her gaze around, taking in the pad, the pen, the room, and finally coming back to Ann. Her eyes had cleared. "Have I been writing?"

Ann said, "Er—may I get you something? Perhaps a cup of tea."

The woman looked down. She was silent for so long that Ann thought she might be going into another trance. Then Elaine said, "A glass of water, please."

"Surely."

"From the bathroom faucet will do."

Ann went into the bathroom. The bath was still full of lightly steaming water. On a tray stretched across it were soap, sponge, and a kitchen knife.

Ann was still looking at the last object when she heard a furtive movement behind her. She whirled. Elaine Scott was in the act of retreating and closing the door. In one hand she held a key. Before Ann could speak or move, the door had closed. Next came the sound of the key being turned in the lock.

Andrew's car was four feet in the air. By one of the rear wheels hunched a mechanic. He was fitting chains around the tyre. Frequently he glanced out of the service bay's window at the falling snow.

Andrew did the same from the public call box in a corner. The flakes, dropping lazily, helped to ease his tension. Even so, he twitched as the telephone rang abruptly. He picked up the receiver.

"Your call to the city is through," the operator said. "Go ahead, please."

It was not only Andrew's impatience that made him keep both preliminaries and call brief; there was a busy man at the other end of the line. The recipient had been Andrew's professor at university and was now in private practice. He said, when Andrew had finished, "I agree one hundred per cent."

Andrew left the booth. The mechanic told him, "You're gonna need these. She's gonna be a good 'un."

"Looks that way," Andrew said absently, his impatience back in full force. He began to pace near the car. He wished he hadn't bothered about getting his tyre chains fitted. He wanted to be on the move.

"How long will this take?" he asked.

"Another fifteen minutes."

"I'll be back." He changed course, went outside and walked away from the gas station.

The falling snow had reduced visibility to forty feet. In some parts the white blobs coasted down gently; in others, blasts of wind drove them into dense, wild swirls.

Trees and rooftops had a smooth coating, as had parked

cars. Roads and sidewalks were, respectively, striped and spotted. There was no humidity: the snow was holding.

Although true dusk was an hour away, the afternoon was dim. Moving vehicles had their headlights on and drove slowly, most of them passing with the thump-thump of tyre chains.

Andrew wondered how many of his telephone calls had been listened to and how long it would take for the goods to spread, be gobbled up or puzzled over. He knew it no longer mattered.

Andrew's hair and shoulders were white by the time he reached the police office. He cleared the flakes off before going in, when he wrinkled his nose at the kerosene smell from the heater even while smiling at its warmth.

The room was small and uncompromisingly functional. Its bleakness had a vaguely threatening air, as though the visitor were already halfway to prison.

Sergeant Stamford rose from his desk. "Hello there. You look as if you could do with a hot coffee."

Andrew's smile turned grateful. "That's the magic word," he said, shucking off his topcoat.

The policeman went to a percolator economically perched atop the heater and filled two tin mugs. "Sorry I don't have a shot of hooch to add."

"The law is the law," Andrew said. "Most of the time." When they were sitting with their coffee he asked what was new on the hit-and-run case.

"Not a thing. I haven't come across so much as a dented fender, although, as I told you yesterday, there doesn't have to be vehicle damage."

"People?"

Tom Stamford shook his head. "Problem there is, *anyone* could've done it. I mean, not one single person had a solid alibi."

Andrew asked, "Do you really think it could have been some farm kid, joyriding his father's truck?"

The sergeant blew steam away from the top of his mug. "You say that as if the idea's the stupidest thing you ever heard."

"Do I?" Andrew said. "I don't mean to sound that way. I think."

"Maybe you have an angle on the case yourself."

"Nope."

With light sarcasm the policeman said, "Or advice as to how I ought to proceed."

Andrew grinned. "Come on, Sarge. I know better than to try and tell a man how to run his own territory."

"Sure. Forget it."

"Let's face it, you people are just like one big family around here."

"In a way."

Andrew drained his mug. Putting it down, he said, "I believe you met my assistant and a friend."

The policeman nodded. "That friend, is she some kind of nut?" While he listened to Andrew talking about Maude Herman's reputed gift, he gazed at the snow spattering against the window. Turning back, he asked:

"So did she learn anything?"

"Perhaps," Andrew said. "I'm still working it out." He got up and stretched, walked to the window and tapped the glass. "There won't be much trick-or-treating tomorrow if this keeps up."

"Could all be gone by the morning. Never can tell."

"In any event, I dare say Halloween's lost a lot of its flavour in Hamlyn Creek after what happened last year."

"Kids forget," the policeman said carelessly.

"But not adults. Even if the case is clean and closed."

Tom Stamford took his mug to the percolator and poured

more coffee. Over his shoulder he said, "What makes you think the case is closed?"

"It has to be."

Stamford turned, sipped, said, "Benny Kaiser was found unfit to plead. If there's no plea, there's no judgement. Officially, the Cissy Scott case is still open."

Andrew asked, "But how do you yourself call it?"

The officer frowned. "Mm?"

"Was the case solved to your satisfaction?"

Tom Stamford looked at him for a long moment. He said, "It wasn't solved at all, far as I'm concerned."

The telephone rang. With a grunt of boredom the policeman sat at his desk and picked up the receiver. After listening, he started to give advice on what stores to get in against the possibility of being snowbound.

Andrew looked at the window as he put on his topcoat. The view of the gloom outdoors was partly obliterated by the blobs of white sticking to the glass. More snow landed and clung while Andrew watched.

Tom Stamford put down the handset with, "You'd think some people'd never seen snow before."

Andrew asked bluntly, "Did Benny kill Cissy Scott?"

"Everyone thinks so but me," the policeman said. "The boy's subnormal. Thinks frightening women is fun."

"What's that got to do with it?"

"Not killer material."

"He confessed," Andrew objected. He felt as if he were arguing against himself.

"That was when I first got hold of him. As you probably know, he took it all back later."

"But you have no proof either way?"

"Not a dime's worth."

The telephone rang again.

"I'll get out of your hair," Andrew said. "Thanks for the

coffee. See you." He opened the door and stepped outside, wincing as the cold blast hit his face. He put his head down and began to walk. Visibility was reduced to thirty feet.

"Hey, Bailey!"

Andrew swung around at the shout. A figure was coming toward him. He recognised Tom Stamford. He went back to meet the police officer, who said in a low, urgent voice:

"That was Harry Scott on the phone. His wife's disappeared."

SEVEN

The tyre chains thumped like a massive heart beating at top speed; the snow was not deep enough yet: the metal links bit through the white layer to the road's hard-top.

The pounding of the chains outraced the rhythm of the Ford's wiper blades, which, shuddering with effort, were keeping two sections of the windshield free of snow.

Andrew drove with severe concentration. He stayed as close as safety allowed to the car in his headlights. He was glad he had caught up with Tom Stamford on the edge of the village. In this weather, and being a near stranger to the district, he knew he could easily lose his way.

His wife's disappeared. That phrase ran repeatedly through Andrew's mind. What exactly did it mean? he wondered. Had she been taken hostage, was she in hiding, had she suddenly vanished into thin air?

Light from behind grew swiftly in strength. It lit the interior of the Ford despite its rear window being blinded with snow. Next came an impatient blast on a horn.

"Stupid bastard," Andrew muttered. "Stay where you are."

The headlights behind shifted their angle. The following moment the car came alongside. Before it went by, Andrew caught a glimpse of the passenger, Rennie Bates, sitting bolt upright, and of the driver, Jack Scott, leaning fiercely over the wheel, his face grim.

The Cadillac swept on past the patrol car and out of sight,

and its wheels threw back slush to spatter heavily on Andrew's windshield. He was forced to slow until the wipers had done their work.

Speeding up again to get close to the police car, he noted that the chains were making less impact and noise. Out here in open country the snow was deeper, and getting more so.

A minute later, after a skidding turn, there was even less noise. The underlying road surface was now dirt.

Andrew shifted his concentration from speed to staying in the tracks left by Tom Stamford's car. He had more traction that way and could benefit from the sergeant's knowledge of the road.

Andrew hummed the tune that was running through his head. He broke off abruptly when, like magic, the patrol car was no longer there. Almost at once Andrew, seeing the gatehouse, realised that Stamford had made a fast turnoff.

Forgetfully, Andrew braked. He gasped as the car went into a spin. He wrenched the steering wheel and released the foot brake. The Ford made one complete, smoothly moving turn and came to a halt level with the private lane.

Andrew lit a cigarette before driving in.

The forecourt was blazing with light. As Andrew stopped, another car arrived from behind him and went into a long slide that almost took it under the carport. Out got Haig Wilson. He hurried into the house. Andrew followed.

The large living room seemed crowded with only eight people. But everyone was restless and talkative. There were Harry and Jack Scott, Ann, Tom Stamford, Mrs. Maynard, Haig Wilson, Rennie Bates, and Andrew himself. Silence fell when the policeman clapped his hands loudly.

"Let's get organised here," he said. "First of all, what's been happening?"

Harry Scott turned to Ann. "You tell it, Miss Goodwin."

Giving most of her attention to Andrew, Ann said, "I

went in the bedroom to see if Mrs. Scott was all right. She seemed fine. She'd had a bath. But she asked me if I'd get her a glass of water. The faucet, she said, would do. I went in the bathroom. Before I could get the water she closed the door. She'd taken the key from the inside."

Tom Stamford asked, "She locked you in?"

"Yes. I knocked and shouted but she didn't answer. And a couple of minutes later I heard the bedroom door close. The window was too small for me to get through, so I pounded on the door. I kept on doing that until Mrs. Maynard heard me."

Jack Scott's manner was rough as he asked the housekeeper, "Did you see Elaine leave?"

The woman, solemn-faced, shook her head. "No, she must've gone out the front door."

"You've searched the house?"

"Of course."

Harry Scott said, "And when I got here—Mrs. Maynard called me at the administration building—we all had another search. In any case, the Cadillac's gone."

The question that Andrew was about to ask was put for him by Sergeant Stamford: "Any of her clothes missing?"

The housekeeper again shook her head. "I checked. Only a pair of jeans and a sweater."

"Could she have gone for a drive?"

"Not in this weather, surely," Haig Wilson said, moving toward the bar. "And not after locking Miss Goodwin in the bathroom. I need a drink. Anyone else? Jack?"

Irritably Jack Scott said, "This is no time for drinking." He ran a hand over his dark hair. "We have to act. I don't like this one little bit."

Harry: "You don't? I'm the one who wanted her in a clinic."

Making his voice deliberately calm, Andrew asked, "How long ago did she leave?"

Ann looked at her watch. "It's thirty minutes since the bathroom door closed on me."

"We're wasting time standing here trying to think of motives," Jack Scott said. "Let's go."

His brother told him, "Another few minutes won't make any difference. We have to plan on what we're going to do. And look, all of you. I'd like to keep this among ourselves for the moment."

Everyone nodded, including the policeman. Rennie Bates said, "It'd make a big splash for the gossips, and, after all, Elaine could come rolling up safely in an hour."

"But why did she get Miss Goodwin out of the way?" Jack asked. "That's what I don't understand."

Sergeant Tom Stamford said, "We'll know that when we find her. Which we will. She won't be doing much travelling today."

"She might not be doing any at all. The Caddy doesn't have chains on."

The housekeeper lifted her hands to her face. "She could've skidded and crashed, hurt herself."

Harry Scott said sharply, "Stop that kind of talk. Let's all keep cool."

Coming from the bar with a drink, Haig Wilson said, "This could be perfectly okay. The bathroom bit, that might have been a whim. Who likes to have a watchdog?"

Harry Scott told him, "Elaine didn't know that Miss Goodwin was here on her account."

"Then it could've been for some other innocuous reason. There always is one. And the disappearance? She might have driven to a pretty spot to have a walk in the snow."

Rennie Bates: "She'd do that."

"She could, in fact, be on the estate someplace."

Jack Scott walked away a few paces, came back. "We're wasting time on chatter."

His brother asked, "What's the best approach to this, Tom?"

The policeman said, "We'll split up and drive off in different directions. Just take any way you fancy. It's too early yet to work by planned sections."

Haig Wilson said, "I'll come with you, Tom, if that's okay. I don't even have snow tyres."

Stamford nodded. "We'll stop cars to ask if anyone's seen the Cadillac, and we'll call home base from time to time, for news. Home base is you, Mrs. Maynard."

The woman acknowledged that with a gesture before saying, "I don't know why she didn't tell me. I would've helped."

"See you," Jack Scott said abruptly. He swung around and strode out of the room.

Rennie Bates called out, "Hey!"

Harry Scott touched her arm. "You can come with me."

"All right."

"And you," Andrew said, "come with me."

Ann gave him a quick smile. There was more in it than the obvious, Andrew realised.

Harry Scott looked at the housekeeper. He said, "The doll."

To the others he added, as the woman was leaving the room, "That's Elaine's lucky charm, companion, talisman, or whatever you might want to call it. A rag doll she's had since she was a girl. She wouldn't make a serious, long-term move without taking that along."

Andrew asked, "What's your true opinion of what your wife's doing?"

Tom Stamford said drily, "If he had one, true or other-

wise, we'd be working on it instead of playing tag around
the countryside."

Mrs. Maynard returned. Her face gave the answer. There
was no need for her to say, "The doll's gone."

The day had aged before its time: full darkness lay beyond the low wall of the forecourt. Here, in the lights, the
snow was dancing prettily, with extra swirls as the other two
cars moved air on driving off. But Ann knew about the cruel
side of snow's nature.

She shivered and was glad when Andrew got in the Ford
after clearing off the windows. He started the motor. "Good
evening, Nurse Goodwin."

"Hello and welcome."

"Did I read the signs correctly in there?"

"I'm sure you did," Ann said.

"So that wasn't the absolute straight story you told."

"Well, I did leave out a couple of things."

Andrew set the car in motion. "I thought so. Good girl.
Did Elaine write?"

"Yes," Ann said, patting the chest of her topcoat. "I have
it in here. I was with her when she did it, luckily. After that
came the bathroom routine."

"That was the truth?"

"The God's honest. What's it all about, Andrew?"

He answered with a question of his own. "What's the
other of the couple of things?"

"A knife. It was on— This isn't the way to the road."

Andrew was turning back from the tarmac lane, whose
black ruts left by the other cars were already filling in with
white. He said, "A hunch. Maybe Elaine went to the old
homestead."

"To hide?"

"For consolation."

"The womb once removed? Yes, good hunch."

"Tell me about the knife."

"Saw edge, kitchen type," Ann said. She explained where she had seen it.

Andrew slowed the car and looked at her. "On the tray?"

"Right. And before I roused dear Mrs. Maynard, I put it in a cupboard. I hope that was right."

"Can't do any harm," Andrew said. He speeded up and peered ahead. "Looks like a car there."

Ann sat on the edge of the seat and put her face close to the windshield. Beside the bulk of the house, a smaller and glittery shape was forming in the Ford's headlights.

"It's a Cadillac," Ann said keenly, but then sat back with a disappointed "Hell." Out of the house had come Jack Scott.

Andrew covered the distance, stopped, and rolled the window down two inches. He called, "Looks as if you had the same hunch that I did."

Jack Scott said, "It didn't work out. No one's been here."

"How about your own house?"

"Harry must've checked it." He opened the door of his car. "But I can try again."

Andrew drove on. "We might as well stay on the estate now we're here," he said. "But back to the writing. Have you read it?"

Ann nodded. "I went over it several times, between sessions of bashing on that damn bathroom door. I did a fair job of decoding, I think."

"It does get easier when you've done it a few times."

"Do you want to read it?"

"No time for that," Andrew said. The tension was apparent in his voice. "I don't want to stop."

"I could take over the wheel," Ann said dubiously. "Or better still, read it to you."

"The gist's good enough. Obviously it isn't the part I'm waiting for, otherwise you'd know."

"Well, it's coming close to the event of last year. A year ago tomorrow. The Halloween thing."

He nodded. "Right."

"You knew that?"

"Yes. Go on."

"The script tells of trying to be cheerful," Ann said. "Of how sad it is that she can't take any enjoyment out of the outing. But she's going to try. There's a lot about the costumes. She's getting dressed up as a witch."

Andrew increased the car's speed. "As you say, sweet, it's right up to the minute."

Ann gripped the seat and the elbow rest as the Ford lurched. They were going along a single-lane track that was only vaguely delineated by white hummocks on either side. The way ahead was virgin snow.

"No one's driven along here," Ann said. "I'm sure of it."

"Hard to tell. Go on about the script."

"That's about all. Oh yes. There's some mention, veiled and unhappy, about *them*—people otherwise unnamed."

Andrew nodded as if disinterested. "No mention of the gun?"

"No, and there's no feeling of premonition."

The car went into a gentle skid, sliding away gracefully off course. Ann tightened her grip until Andrew, slowing, had regained control and had the tyre chains biting.

She said, "It seems to me that the president of the Ontario Society for Psychical Research is holding a lot back from his trusted assistant."

Andrew gave her a brief smile, patted her knee. "You're right, he is. He's not positive yet. Please be patient."

"In other words, 'All in good time, my dear.' You sound infuriatingly like my father."

Andrew lifted one shoulder in a semi-shrug. Ann said, "Please tell me one thing. Is Elaine Scott in real danger?"

"Yes, Ann. Very much so."

"Oh."

Andrew took the car at speed over a rise in the unseen track. It levelled with a suddenness that made Ann's stomach quail and leap. Holding onto her supports, she decided against distracting Andrew with any more talk.

Presently they came to a T-junction. The crossing road had tyre ruts in the snow, an intermingling of brown and black lines. Stopping, Andrew said:

"This is the edge of the O'Neal spread. I think we might as well leave it behind."

"So do I," Ann agreed with relief. "Left or right?"

"You choose."

Before she could do so, headlights came into view, seen merely as a brightness beyond the falling snowflakes. Andrew began to get out, saying, "I'll do the asking bit." He went and stood in the middle of the road, waving his arms.

With old Jim Webber in mind, Ann clenched her toes. She relaxed when the approaching vehicle, a panel truck, came to a slithery stop. Andrew spoke to the driver, came back to the Ford and got in.

"The man's just left his farm," he said, wiping snow off his hair. "We're the first car he's seen."

"Was he curious?"

"He's going to the doctor with earache. That's his only interest at the moment."

They drove on, taking the direction the van had come from. The car windows were clear of snow only at the front, where the wiper blades groaned busily. The blobs of white were large and numerous and falling at speed.

Ann suggested, "Isn't it time we checked with Mrs. Maynard?"

"You're right. Next place we come to."

"Which reminds me." She told what the housekeeper had said about Andrew's telephone call from Jim Webber's. "I hope the old bat doesn't get you in trouble."

Andrew said, "I couldn't care less."

It was ten minutes before a house appeared. They had seen no other vehicles in that time, except a small foreign car abandoned on the shoulder of the road.

Ann went to the house. Its owners, a young couple, seemed to find her request perfectly reasonable, and she was able to make the call without rousing their curiosity. After identifying herself on the telephone she asked a cryptic, "Anything?" The answer was equally to the point: "No."

They went on driving. Even with the heater going at full blast, Ann felt chilled, the world outside was so silent and lonely. The snow had no charm under the present circumstances.

The car's lurching was no help, nor was Andrew's almost surly grimness. Once when Ann spoke to him he turned to her as if coming back from a thousand miles away and asked, "What?"

Headlights appeared. When they began to flash up and down, from full to dim and back, Andrew slowed. He stopped as the other car came alongside. The driver said:

"Have you seen . . . Oh, it's you."

It was Tom Stamford, with Haig Wilson in the passenger seat. Andrew told them, "We've had no luck, and there's no news at the house. You?"

"Well," the policeman said, "we did find where a car had been parked off the road. By the tyre marks, I'd say it could've been a Caddy. Right, Haig?"

The sports writer leaned forward. "Right. And there were tracks in the snow leading away from it. But the funniest damn tracks you ever saw."

Stamford: "It was like someone walking sideways on his feet and hands, or maybe trailing a stick out to the side."

Andrew asked, "You followed?"

"Naturally. They wandered around and finished back at where the car had been."

"Could've been Elaine," Haig Wilson said. "But those tracks, I don't figure it."

Ann said, "She could have been writing in the snow."

"Yes," Andrew said a minute later as they were driving on. "That could well be the answer."

"Writing one continuous line, moving along in a crouch."

"And whatever she wrote she would unthinkingly have wiped out with her supporting left hand as she went."

"If not," Ann said, "the snow will have nicely taken care of it by now."

Andrew grunted. He thought for a while before asking, "In the script you have there, is Elaine still in the house?"

"Yes, it ends with her saying something along the lines of them looking like a pair of ghosts, enough to frighten some poor child out of its wits."

Andrew felt a shade easier. But he knew it was a question of time. Though the scripts were, of course, less important than the safety of Elaine Scott. That was a matter of time as well.

Andrew wished he were alone so that he could release a string of obscenities at the snow. He also wished he could go the other way, be more civilised, bring himself to act nicer to Ann. But his mood was too black, his nerves too taut.

He leaned forward, staring at the way ahead. He had no idea where they were. The whiteness in the headlights seemed no different from any of the other patches of countryside he had seen since the search began.

Ann lit two cigarettes, one of which she put in Andrew's

lips. "Thanks, sweet," he said. "I'll apologise later for being such poor company."

"Don't worry."

"Listen. Why don't we get engaged?"

"Well now, there's a notion," Ann said. "I'm not doing anything at the moment."

"And therefore?"

"Lovely," she said, opening her pocketbook. She brought out a ring and put it on. She held up her hand. "Pretty?"

"Great," Andrew said.

"I brought it with me this morning. Lifted it from your shirt drawer. You always get romantic toward the end of a case."

"Some Romeo I am."

"You'll do," Ann said, sliding closer.

Although Andrew realised it would be crass of him not to stop the car and embrace Ann, he went on driving. Ann would know she was kissing someone whose mind was ninety per cent elsewhere.

He said, "Remind me to buy you something very expensive and very frivolous."

"That I promise to do," Ann said. In a different tone she asked, "Isn't that the gatehouse?"

Andrew peered. "It is."

"You know, for a while there I thought we were lost."

He laughed. "Really?"

"We keep going, of course."

"Of course. We'll have to give it two or three hours."

Ann said, "The first one's nearly up."

Now that he had his bearings, and because he had paid special attention on previous occasions, Andrew recognised the segment of roadside that was growing in his headlights. It was the patch of trees where Elaine and Cissy Scott had made their first—and final—stop on Halloween a year ago.

Andrew identified the place for Ann as he drew off the road there. She asked, "Another hunch?"

"No, a whim. But I can call Mrs. Maynard from the farmhouse. It's about time." He stopped the car. "Will you be all right here?"

"With the doors locked, yes. I don't care if they do say lightning never strikes twice in the same place."

Andrew stubbed his cigarette, took a flashlight from under the dashboard and got out of the car. He heard the lock click firmly into place.

The snow came over his ankles as he moved to the front of the car. By its lights he saw his way to plod up the rise. The going was slippery. At the top, he switched his flash on.

He gasped at the crashing that sounded right beside him. Swinging around, he saw that it had been a heap of snow falling from a branch. He blew out a burst of vapour and went on, down the incline.

Dimly through the falling snow he could make out the lights of the house. He told himself it formed a pretty picture, but he wasn't in the mood. And his nerves nipped again as more snow crashed from a tree.

The next thing Andrew heard brought him to a halt. It was the sound of a car door closing. He looked all around but, because of the snow, sound direction was uncertain.

He turned. His car was out of sight, over the hillock. He stood still, listening. It was incredibly silent, as though he had been stricken with total deafness, or as if the world were stunned with surprise. He clicked his tongue to make a noise.

Then he straightened. He had heard voices which lingered in the air. Again, direction was unsure. But he could hear enough to know that it was a man and a woman talking.

Andrew began to hurry back to the Ford. Haste made

him slip. He fell to one knee, leapt up, went on. He slipped twice more before reaching the top of the rise.

Gasping, he stopped there. Below, he could make out the car, and Ann inside, and a tall thin man talking to her. Andrew blew out a heavy burst of vapour and began a slow descent.

When closer he played his flashlight over the man, who flinched away from the glare and said, "Hey, watch that."

As Andrew lowered the flash he noticed a car standing some distance away on the road.

Ann, her window open half an inch, said, "This man's looking for the Scott house. Do we know where that is?"

Andrew arrived at the Ford. The tall man wore a jazzy-hued lumberjack coat and a skiing cap. He was about forty and had a grin that seemed permanent, as well as supercilious.

"Great weather," he said.

Andrew looked at him closely. "I've seen you before somewhere."

"Maybe. You look familiar too. I'm Hank Tillotsen of the Toronto *Star*."

"Sure," Andrew said. He introduced himself. "We've seen each other around."

The reporter's grin widened. "The plot thickens."

"It does?"

"Funniest damn thing, Bailey. I stop a patrol car a few minutes ago to ask the way. He's a local cop, I know that, I saw him in these parts a year ago. But do you think he knows where the Scott house is?"

"No?" Andrew said innocently.

"No way. He shook his head and drove on. The other guy with him, he wouldn't even turn and look at me. It begins to smell real good."

"What begins to smell good?"

"Listen," Hank Tillotsen said. "Tonight I get a telephone tip. Hot, the guy tells me. Get out to the Harry Scotts' near Hamlyn Creek. On the double. I know by the voice that something's on, even though the thrill tone could be phonied. But I come. Hell, news is slow. First that hick cop gives me the brush, now I find our spook expert in the vicinity. Smells like a story."

Andrew said, "I'm visiting a sick uncle."

"And I'm King Henry X."

The road whitened as it was lit by an approaching car's headlights. Ann opened the door. She said, "I'll flag those people down. See if they can give us a bearing."

Andrew added, "We're lost ourselves, Tillotsen."

"Aw, come on."

"Tell me, what were you doing here a year ago?"

"I'll give you one hundred guesses."

"Okay, okay," Andrew said. "And this is the very spot where it happened."

The reporter looked around. "Jesus, I really am lost. If it wasn't for this snow, I'd easy find my way."

"Why don't you tell me about your hot tip? Who was it?"

Hank Tillotsen laughed and shook his head. "No getee, no givee. You know the rules, Bailey."

Andrew looked over at the road, where Ann, having stopped a truck, was talking to the driver. Thoughtfully Andrew got out cigarettes, lit one and had it sizzle out at once, hit on the cinder by a snowflake. He threw the cigarette away.

"Okay," he said, turning to the reporter. "I'll make a deal with you. You tell me about your call and then fade. Later I'll give you everything you want on the story—if there is one."

"There is one."

"We don't know that for sure. But anyway, what do you

say? And look, no one's going to give you anything on your own, not tonight. You'll get more brushes than Fuller. Meeting me now could be the best thing that's happened to you this year."

"Tell you what, Bailey," the reporter said. "I'll fade as far as the hotel in Hamlyn Creek. If I don't hear from you in a couple of hours, I snoop."

Ann came back—the truck had driven on—and with an enigmatic smile got in the car. Andrew said:

"Tillotsen, you have a deal. But you don't have to tell me anything. I'll tell you. Just answer yes or no. Okay?"

"Check."

"The hot-tip call was anonymous, male, and came"—looking at his watch—"fifty-five minutes ago."

The reporter also looked at his watch. He said, "Yes, yes, and fifty-seven minutes."

"That's good enough. See you at the hotel."

"I'll be in the bar," Tillotsen said, walking off.

Andrew went around and got inside the car. As soon as the door was closed Ann said breathlessly, "That was Harry Scott and Rennie in the truck. They just called the house. Jack's found Elaine."

The reason Ann gripped her supports tightly as the car sped along was not now because of fearing an accident but out of excitement. She had found it unbearable, having to act calm until the reporter was out of the way.

Ann's face was as set and keen as Andrew's. She didn't even flicker her eyelids when the car went into a slide while taking a corner.

Andrew counterwised the steering wheel, the tyre chains bit down, the car straightened out. The next minute they were turning again, by the gatehouse. The private lane was striped black and white, like a mammoth trouser leg.

"Now of all times," Ann said. She was referring to the appearance of Hank Tillotsen.

"That," Andrew said, "is the point."

"What?"

But now they were at the forecourt. Within two minutes they were taking off their topcoats in the living room and answering the quietly satisfied greetings of the others.

At the bar stood Tom Stamford and Haig Wilson, with Rennie Bates between them on a stool. Jack Scott was playing bartender. He said in answer to Andrew's question:

"In the bedroom. Harry and Mrs. Maynard are getting her out of her wet clothes."

"Is she all right?"

"I think so. Come and have a warmer."

Ann and Andrew joined the others. Sergeant Tom Stamford said, "So go on, Jack. You saw the Caddy in this drift."

"On a back road about eight miles from here," Jack Scott recapped for the newcomers, handing them glasses of whiskey. "Elaine had been stuck there for some time, trying to get out. The tyres were still smoking."

Haig Wilson: "She was in the car?"

"Right. I guess she'd finally given up trying, though the motor was still running."

"She'd need that for the heater," the policeman said. "What did she say?"

"Nothing. She was in a trance. She'd just gone into it."

Standing beside Andrew, Ann had felt him tense up, though his voice was normal as he asked, "How d'you know that—that the trance had only just started?"

Jack Scott sipped his drink, lowered the glass. "Because she was writing with her finger on the fogged-up window, and there were only half a dozen words."

Ann sensed Andrew's tension toning down. She said, "Did you let her go on?"

"Hell, no. I got her out of there and into my own car."

Rennie Bates said, "It's supposed to be dangerous, waking people out of trances."

"That may be so," Jack Scott said. "But worse to leave her sitting there in wet clothes."

"I guess. But how did she get wet in the first place?"

While the policeman and Haig Wilson were explaining about the tracks they had found, Harry Scott came through the arch. At the bar he was handed a glass of whiskey, which he downed at a single gulp. When the others had finished he said:

"I wonder if we should get the doctor to her."

His brother said, "Wouldn't hurt."

Haig Wilson shook his head. "For a chill, you couldn't drag out even a kin doctor on a night like this."

"Of course not," Andrew said. He took Ann's glass away from her. "Nurse Goodwin will take a look."

Ann nodded. "Certainly." She moved away.

Tom Stamford said, "Tell you another funny thing. We were stopped by a guy that Haig knows. He was looking for this house. He's a reporter from the city."

Ann, leaving the room, heard to her confusion Andrew joining in with the others' exclamations of surprise. She went on to the sleeping quarters.

Elaine Scott, wearing a robe and a scarf, was sitting up in bed, propped by pillows, her head resting back and her eyes closed. Somehow the look of exhaustion added to her beauty.

Mrs. Maynard came to Ann. Nervously she whispered, "I made her take two aspirins and some brandy with hot water. I hope that was all right."

"Can't do any harm. Does she have a temperature?"

"I don't know."

"Let's check."

The woman put out a hand. "Don't wake her up, please. She's just dozed off."

Ann said, speaking softly, "There's no hurry. And I'm sure she's perfectly well. A cold, at the worst. She wasn't in the snow long enough to get a thorough chilling. And the car was well heated."

The housekeeper, her eyes intent on Ann's face, had been nodding at the words as if in thanks for a gift. Ann was touched by the implied devotion. She helped by asking about the patient's medical history. With obvious enjoyment, Mrs. Maynard began a recounting of ailments, starting with an attack of measles at the age of eight.

Her nervousness had settled by the time Harry Scott and Andrew appeared in the doorway. The former asked about his wife. Ann told him she was fine, adding:

"Rest and warmth, that's probably all she needs."

"But I think I'll have the doctor come out tomorrow, anyway."

"Of course. It's best to be sure."

"Is she sleeping now?" Harry Scott asked.

Ann said, "Yes."

Andrew looked past her. "Are you certain?"

Ann turned toward the bed. Elaine Scott was the same as before, except that now her right hand was making small, furtive movements. Ann glanced back as she heard Rennie Bates say, "It's a trance." The others from the living room had arrived.

Andrew came briskly into the room. Within seconds he had given a pad and pen to the woman on the bed. Immediately Elaine Scott began to write. Faint frowns twitched across her forehead like responses to mild pain.

Andrew backed off. He stood near the foot of the bed. Though his expression was bland, Ann knew it was a façade. He was keeping his triumph carefully under cover.

Turning away from the bed, he looked at everyone present. He said, "I think this is a good moment for me to explain what's happening. Explain these so-called trances."

Involuntarily, Ann drew in a breath in preparation for speaking, at the same time swaying forward. She checked herself.

"To begin with," Andrew said, "the trances have nothing to do with the occult. They are not psychic."

Ann was unable to hold back a slow "What?"

Harry Scott asked, "What are you talking about?"

Andrew said, "I've seen hundreds of self-induced trances. Any good medium can produce one at will. Mrs. Scott's I recognised as different the first time I saw it, though its real nature had me puzzled. I finally got what I thought was the right diagnosis, and today called an analyst associate in the city. He agreed with me when I told him the symptoms and circumstances."

Harry Scott, looking at his wife, who was still writing, said, "I'm not with you, Bailey."

Andrew nodded toward the bed. "What you're seeing is a psychological condition, not psychic, and one that's by no means uncommon. Mrs. Scott, in fact, is in a catatonic state. It was induced by tension, hysteria."

The following silence was broken by Sergeant Tom Stamford. He asked, "So who's been making Elaine write?"

"No one," Andrew said. "Not her grandmother or anyone else. The scripts are the work of Mrs. Scott."

EIGHT

Andrew, standing with his back to the imitation fire, looked around the living room. Everyone was here with the exception of Mrs. Maynard and Elaine Scott. The older woman was staying with the younger, who, when her writing was finished, had fallen asleep. She had worn a sad smile.

Ann and Rennie Bates sat on a couch that faced the hearth, with the police officer straddling one of its arms. Harry Scott was standing to the rear of the nearby easy chair his brother was sitting in. Haig Wilson, on a tall stool, leaned back with both elbows on the bar. Everyone looked mystified and expectant.

Andrew was not unaware of his enjoyment at being the centre of avid attention. He had not expected this public unravelling of the affair; he had been prepared to write out the usual report, sending one copy to the Scotts, one to the Director of Public Prosecutions, and adding a third to OSPR's files.

But with him this was fine, as was the fact that it was happening today: he had presumed that the last instalment would not be forthcoming until tomorrow.

One or two of Andrew's audience shuffled impatiently. He said, "Quite apart from my doubts about the trance state, I suspected from the beginning that it wasn't Moina O'Neal talking through the pen of Mrs. Scott."

Ann cleared her throat. Avoiding looking at her, Andrew went on, "The writer talked of her hair showing up against black velvet. Although white in later years, Moina was dark when younger. And it was explicit in the scripts that it was a young woman talking."

Andrew told of finally proving the suspicion by the date of the church clock installation. "We next thought of the later Cissy Scott, thought that she might sometime have dyed her hair blond. If she had, I didn't learn of it in asking around."

Jack Scott put his glass on the floor between his feet. He said, "My wife had never dyed her hair. Neither during nor before our marriage."

"Quite," Andrew said. "And I today got solid proof that Mrs. Scott was the real source of the scripts by telephoning the county old folks' home. The writer had mentioned sending clothes there anonymously. One such donation did arrive there the summer before last."

Sergeant Stamford said, "Okay, the writing is by Elaine herself. That, I would agree, has been well and truly established. So what?"

"Yes," Haig Wilson added. "You act as though you were holding an inquest or something."

Andrew reached behind him and lifted several pages from the mantelshelf. "I want you all to hear the latest script, which could easily be the last."

Harry Scott took his hands out of his pockets. "You mean Elaine's cured of all this stuff?"

"Possibly. I can't see any reason, in fact, why she shouldn't be. Not after this."

Harry looked dubious. "You make it sound very simple."

Andrew flapped the pages. "I'm going to read this aloud. Or rather, Rennie and I are going to read it. We'll alternate."

The policeman sighed his impatience. He asked, "Why the double act, Bailey?"

"Well, I take it that you all trust our Miss Bates?"

The four men nodded, and Jack Scott said, "Absolutely."

"Fine," Andrew said. "So if Rennie reads the script with me, you'll know it's a true reading. You won't think I'm putting bits in or, equally important, leaving bits out."

Harry Scott said, "That's fair enough." He brought forward an upright chair, turned it, sat on it in reverse alongside his brother.

Andrew asked the secretary, "You don't mind doing this?"

"I'm delighted," Rennie Bates said, getting up and coming forward. "Not to mention fascinated."

Haig Wilson called, "Don't be too hammy, Ren."

The girl giggled. She stood beside Andrew with her back to the fire. They held the script between them like a shared hymnbook.

Andrew, having already gone over the wording to get the gist, knew what to expect, therefore knew that the banter and light mood, created by the euphoria at Elaine having been found safely, would soon fade from the scene. But the sooner the better, he thought.

To that end Andrew said, "I should perhaps preface this by telling about the most recent scripts. They've been coming at a faster rate, and they've been bringing us right up to date, as of one year ago. One year ago tomorrow night."

He looked from person to person as that sank in. There was a shifting in the positions of bodies. Everyone stared.

Rennie Bates seemed to ease away from him slightly. Haig Wilson slowly lost the carefree smile he had been showing, while Jack Scott appeared to grow a shade more appreciative. His brother looked offended. The police officer's frown could have been caused by anger or jealousy.

The only verbal response came from him. He said, "You better explain that."

Andrew tapped the pages. "This is the best explanation," he said. "Listen, please." He began to read aloud:

"And as we turned by the gatehouse I felt cheerful. All the ugliness was forgotten for the moment. Being dressed up was fun. I didn't know why I hadn't looked forward to the outing. I told myself I had to get back among the living. I made a joke and we both laughed."

Andrew touched Rennie Bates with his elbow. She coughed and took over the reading.

"A few minutes later I steered off the road to make the first call. We had agreed it would be mine. I stopped the car and we both got out. We met at the back, to open the trunk and get out a box of favours. And it was then that it happened. Out of nowhere. Over nothing. Cissy made an innocent remark, and I exploded."

Andrew read out:

"It all came up like boiling lava. Everything I'd kept down in the depths for months. All the rage and sadness, all the pain and ego damage, all the battered emotions of a woman scorned and cheated. I began to rant at Cissy. Told her I knew everything. Threw out every clue I'd discovered. Called her every filthy name I could think of, for her having an affair with my husband."

Andrew waited for Rennie to take over the reading. She did not. She raised her head. Andrew did the same.
Harry Scott had his fists together, gripping the chair back.

His face was pale. As motionless and silent as everyone else in the room, he was staring at the floor but away to the right. His brother was on his left.

Jack Scott had his eyes closed. He wore no expression. Slowly he let himself sink back in the easy chair. His feet came together and knocked his drink over.

The next movement came from the arch. Elaine Scott appeared there, though it was patent that she had taken only this one step, had been standing out of sight. Behind her was Mrs. Maynard.

Harry Scott glanced back, then, slowly, turned to the front again. He broke the room's aching silence with one word, his wife's name. After a moment he added:

"I didn't know you knew."

Elaine Scott stayed in the arch. Her face was calm. She was looking at Sergeant Tom Stamford. Softly she said, "It doesn't matter now."

Harry's eyes kept going from right to left. "It matters," he said, his voice husky. "I love you."

"All right."

"We have to talk about this. Later."

The silence was back. Elaine went on looking at the police officer. Mrs. Maynard hovered protectively close.

Andrew cleared his throat. He said, "I'd like to go on with this script, if nobody objects."

Elaine Scott said, "Please do, Mr. Bailey."

Andrew nudged Rennie Bates. She shook her head, which she had lowered, moved away, and returned to her place on the couch, sitting heavily.

Lifting the pages, Andrew read out:

"It might have been all right but for Cissy's attitude. She began to talk as if humouring a child. She said I should try and be more mature about these things. That kind of talk. I was still ranting. I opened the door and got the gun from under the front seat. I think I wanted to frighten her, or make her be quiet, or show her that my feelings were real, and deep, not petty. I was heart-broken and here she was acting as if I were a foolish prude, snapping about trifles."

Andrew turned to the last page, reading aloud:

"She came at me. We struggled. We staggered back and forth. She was frightened. So was I. Cissy called for help, she shouted at me to be sensible, she promised to break it off with Harry. In a fury of panic she began to fight for possession of the gun. I hit my head against the car. I heard the gun going off. I didn't believe any-thing that was happening. But it was true. My dizziness cleared, and there she was on the ground, the front of her costume red with blood. I felt her pulse. She was dead."

Andrew lifted his head. Reaching behind him, he put the script on the mantelshelf. "The rest of it we know," he said. "Mrs. Scott covered up by going to the farm."

If the silence in the room had ached before, now it pained fiercely. Jack Scott had not opened his eyes; had, in fact, closed them more tightly. His sister-in-law was still looking at the policeman, a fatalistic gaze. Haig Wilson had slowly got off the bar stool and was standing in a bewildered stoop.

Tom Stamford, his freckles standing out on a face that was whiter than normal, had his face turned toward Mrs. Scott but his eyes averted. Rennie Bates held both hands to her mouth. Ann's gape at Andrew was as disbelieving as Harry Scott's.

The latter said, "You're mad."

"I? I'm only the reader."

Over his shoulder Harry asked, "Is that what you wrote?"

Tonelessly his wife said, "I imagine so. That's the way it happened."

"You mean it's true?"

"Yes."

Harry Scott went on gaping, the way all the others seemed incapable of changing, of rousing themselves to action or speech.

Andrew said, "From that time on, Mrs. Scott's emotional turmoil began. It grew worse as the anniversary of the killing approached. She suffered and feared."

Andrew recalled his first inkling of what could have taken place. It had been in the old homestead parlour, when Elaine reacted violently to her husband taking her by the wrists—the symbolic manacles.

He went on, "Mrs. Scott's agony had many edges. She was wretched that an innocent youth should be in an institution for the criminally insane, and she was horrified at what she had done, yet at the same time she dreaded the results of what her conscience was urging her to do—confess.

"The guilt over Benny Kaiser and her own act, the dread and the urging, created massive tension. This increased as the anniversary neared. The tension caused catatonic states. They were an escape, a temporary out. But in these abstractions she gave in to her moral side.

"At first the writings were as much an apologia as a confession. She was explaining herself. She was trying to show that she was a decent, ordinary person. Then hints of the affair started to creep into the scripts. Aware of what was happening, of what she would eventually say in the writing, she became more than ever an object of tension and despair."

Andrew paused. He said, "And it was all so unnecessary."

Everyone looked at him. He added, "Elaine Scott did not kill Cissy."

Ann's feeling of shock ended, just as its preceding emotion, acute embarrassment, had also faded. Before that, there had been a period of annoyance: at Andrew, for having kept her so completely in the dark. She had soon realised, however, that much of this was because of the non-occult causation of the occurrences.

But was that totally so? Ann wondered now. Could not the writing have been prompted by the dead, Moina O'Neal or Cissy, who, knowing Elaine to be innocent, were pushing for her to escape despair? It was possible.

Ann's embarrassment had stemmed from her being present at a public washing of dirty linen, the family secret exposed. The atmosphere had been desperate. A saving grace had been that, from her place on the couch, Ann could see none of those involved. She had held her eyes firmly on Andrew.

Sergeant Tom Stamford repeated ploddingly, "Elaine Scott did not kill Cissy."

Andrew: "That's right."

The policeman gave a harsh laugh. "So what in hell have you dragged all this stuff out for?"

"It has to be told."

"Why, Bailey?"

Andrew said, "Because it's part of the solution."

"Is Elaine innocent or not?"

"Yes," Andrew said. He looked toward the arch. "Mrs. Scott, there was no need for those attempts at suicide."

Ann heard a general intake of breath, like a sigh of wind, plus Haig Wilson's muttered "Jesus."

"No need," Andrew said, "for you to try and kill yourself

that night in the kitchen. Although, of course, the explosion had nothing to do with a pressure cooker."

Elaine Scott said, "No."

"Our lab ran a test on that. But I imagine Mrs. Maynard was more than willing to help you with a lie. Right?"

The housekeeper asked a defiant "Why shouldn't I?" and Elaine Scott said with a new tone in her voice, a faint but distinct vibrancy:

"It was the gas stove. I opened the oven door, lay there and turned on the gas. But I couldn't go through with it. I turned the tap off and went back to my room. That's when the explosion happened."

Tom Stamford said, "Gas is heavier than air, but it finally rose high enough to meet the pilot light on top of the stove."

Andrew nodded. "Exactly."

"If you knew all this before, why . . ."

Andrew ignored him. "And in the bath tonight, Mrs. Scott, did you plan on slashing your wrists with that knife?"

Haig Wilson again said, "Jesus." Ann could feel the shudder that ran through Rennie Bates.

Elaine said, "It was an idea. I was going to try. But I didn't. I lacked the courage."

"You ran away instead," Andrew said. "All unnecessary, but all part of the pressure."

Elaine Scott asked, "Is it true what you're saying, Mr. Bailey? Am I really innocent? Can it be possible?"

Andrew folded his arms. "Mrs. Scott, I doubt if you could kill, yourself or anyone else. You're not the type. That shows in you and in your writing. Never once when you were suspecting the love affair, nor when it was proven, did murder occur to you."

As earlier, Ann's upper body moved forward involuntarily. She stopped herself in time from interrupting. But Andrew had got the message. He went on:

"You did, Mrs. Scott, sense an atmosphere of death. Probably that is the one paranormal connection in this case. What you were feeling, through extrasensory perception, was the intention, the murder plan being formed in the killer's mind."

Sergeant Stamford asked an irritable "Plan?"

"Exactly. The killer planned it and brought it off. It was all wrapped up beautifully. But then he began to get worried that it might not stay quiet. You, Mrs. Scott, might remember, you might even have seen him. Benny Kaiser might come up with an alibi. There was the killer's own alibi. And there was the matter of the gun."

Ann heard a movement from the direction of the bar, followed by a clinking of glass. Beside her, Rennie Bates sat in a huddle, hands tucked tight under her armpits.

"The killer was very happy when these writings began," Andrew said. "He saw what they were and hoped they were leading to a confession. He knew Mrs. Scott must believe herself guilty, otherwise she wouldn't have covered up the way she did. If she confessed, he would be really safe.

"He suggested the Ontario Society for Psychical Research, an official body. To be on the safe side, he arranged for me what appeared to be a ghostly visitation by Moina O'Neal. It seemed as if someone was trying to scare me off, but it was actually to stimulate my interest."

Ann was too intrigued to be irked by this destruction of one of her prize pieces. She listened carefully.

Andrew went on, "The killer said it was pointless to try and keep the story of the trances from the locals. He was hoping the word would spread—but he hadn't counted on the locals' closed-mouth attitude with outsiders. The point is, he wanted the media to know, just as he wanted an official body involved, because he wanted to abnegate the possibility of a hush-up when the confession finally came—

by both the family and the police. He knew, as did every-one, that Tom Stamford had once been attracted to Elaine Scott, and perhaps still was."

The police officer said blurtingly, "Now hold on there."

Andrew didn't. He continued, "Tonight, with the scripts coming fast, and Elaine gone, the killer panicked. He made an anonymous call to a reporter, one who had covered the murder case last year. Timewise, only one person could have made that call, the same person who showed no further in-terest in the reason for the ghostly visitation, the same per-son who spread the rumour that was groundless, that no old-timer I talked to had ever heard of—the story of Moina O'Neal's hidden treasure."

Haig Wilson asked, "What was the point of that?"

"To explain his reason for encouraging the trances," An-drew said. He turned toward Harry Scott. "I'd like you to tell me something."

The host's voice was lifeless. "Well?"

"You and Jack always did things in pairs. Twin houses, cars and trucks alike, gadgets the same. On that trip to the States two years ago, you didn't buy one gun, did you? You bought two. You each bought an identical revolver."

"Well, yes," Harry said. "That's right."

"But after the murder Jack asked you to keep quiet about his gun. Naturally. He told you he didn't want a fine and confiscation. Right?"

"I—I don't have to answer that."

"You have," Andrew said. He looked at Jack Scott. "That's been your biggest worry all along. The gun. The gun that never killed anyone, yet it explains how you killed your wife."

Haig Wilson, behind the bar, froze in the act of pouring out another drink. The police officer slowly rose from the arm of the couch, his right hand simultaneously sinking to his holster, though that movement seemed more protective than aggressive.

Rennie Bates huddled still deeper into herself, as if trying to grow smaller. Ann looked as though she were having a hard time containing questions, her lips pressed together.

Harry Scott was staring at the hands that gripped the chair back close to his face. He was losing his colour, the flush that had appeared with Andrew's last words.

Elaine Scott had not moved from the arch. She was leaning weakly against its side. Her mouth was slightly open, her gaze sad-dreamy. She was like someone who, in a short space of time, had gone through every emotion possible and now was devoid of feeling.

The middle-aged woman standing to the rear of Elaine wore an expression of smug satisfaction.

Jack Scott looked paralysed. He sat motionless in the easy chair. His head was back, his arms were straight down, with the hands limp beside his thighs. In a face that seemed to have aged, his eyes showed the only signs of animation. They slowly roved floor, walls, ceiling—anywhere except near the man standing in front of the fireplace.

Andrew said, "I don't know which of two motives made you want to kill Cissy. Rage and hate at her cheating, or fear that Elaine might find out about it. That, the second, could have been disastrous for you. Here you had a luxurious perch, a life of ease. There was the danger of Elaine divorcing Harry, which would have meant you were out as well.

"There could, of course, have been another motive altogether. Was there?"

Jack Scott appeared to be finding a corner of the room of reasonable interest. The others were silent and still.

"Your plan was medium good," Andrew went on. "I've

known better. There had been a woman-molester in the neighbourhood, so it's suggested that the girls take a gun along on their Halloween outing. For safety, the first chamber in the revolver will have a blank in it. That Cissy got from the theatre. On the night in question, you yourself did the loading. You did not, however, put in one blank. You put in six. After all, you wouldn't want to risk getting shot yourself.

"This was neat and safe. Should it be discovered, before the girls left the house, that the gun held nothing but duds, you could always claim to have disliked the thought of them having a loaded weapon.

"The other blanks you got from the same source—the theatre. Neat again. No worry about a purchase being unearthed later. But unfortunately there's no explanation for so many to be missing from the one box of blanks I examined in the theatre prop room. It's the only box sold to the group by your local hardware dealer eighteen months ago. He remembers it because he had to order it especially. And from Claud Trubolt I learned that no plays in that time had the need of blank cartridges, though one such play had been planned."

As Andrew paused, there came a tinkling noise from the bar. Haig Wilson was shakily pouring out a drink. Looking up, he put the bottle and glass down.

Andrew said to Jack Scott, "You left the house before your wife and your sister-in-law. You said you were going to play cards with old Jim Webber. Which is what you did. You'd done it many times before, and often the old man had fallen asleep. In fact he nearly dozed off the first time I myself played cribbage with him. And he did so on my next visit. It was the reason I went there, though he thought I was after gossip and information.

"Perhaps on Halloween you helped Jim along with a sedative or a strong drink. That would have been a sensible move. But in any case, with him being the type who hated to be thought old, you knew he'd rather lose a leg than own up to napping."

Sergeant Tom Stamford, one hand still on his holster, made a movement as if about to speak. Then he said quietly, "Never mind. Go on with it."

"When you heard the Cadillac go by the gatehouse," Andrew said, "or maybe before, depending on Jim's consciousness or otherwise, you left and ran over the fields to the girls' first stop. You would, naturally, have done the run before, timed it. You expected to be gone some fifteen minutes at most.

"On arrival at the parked car, you got a surprise. You must have been astounded when Elaine started to rage at Cissy for having an affair with your brother. You hadn't been aware that Elaine knew. But, not being a fool, she had seen the same clues and signs that you had over the past months."

Andrew shook his head. "I can imagine how you felt at that moment. You must have been profoundly sorry that you hadn't loaded the gun with real shells, even though there was still the question of Harry and you being pushed out into the cold. But you had your own gun along, the twin of the other. It *was* loaded with one blank shell and five real bullets."

The police officer nodded. "Sure."

Andrew told Jack Scott, "You went through with it. You didn't wait for shooting or for the argument and struggle to run down—although, of course, you couldn't have guessed how it was going to turn out, with Elaine thinking herself guilty. You sneaked quickly up behind her and hit her on the head. What was said between you and your wife only you know. It couldn't have been much, if anything. Time was too short. You shot her, dropped your gun by Elaine, and pulled the other out of her hand. You ran back to old Jim's. There everything was fine. Mission accomplished."

Andrew sighed. He felt tired. He had begun to lose his urgency in ratio to the growing tension and alertness of the others in the room, with the main exception of Jack Scott himself, who was the epitome of inertia.

Andrew told him, "Everything was going for you. Elaine told a different story, a young man was put away for the shooting, you were not even remotely suspected. To all intents and purposes, the case was closed. But you worried about it. You drank too much, and worried about that as well, thinking people might start to wonder. It was a great day for you when Elaine started her automatic writing."

Sergeant Stamford said, "And that's where you and your society came in. From there we know it. Almost. What about Jim Webber?"

Andrew nodded. "Jack Scott's alibi loomed important again when I began to spend some time with Jim. So Jim had to die too. How Scott killed him I don't know. It was clean and clever. I do know Jim was called outside, supposedly for only a minute. He had left his nearly cooked potatoes boiling."

Andrew looked at Jack Scott. "Perhaps you asked him to stand in the road and look at your car as it approached. You wanted him to see if a wheel was shaky. Something like that. Maybe you reversed into him. Those being risky— someone could've happened along—perhaps before taking him to the roadside you rendered him unconscious and then dropped a rock on his back."

He gave a polite semi-bow. "Would you care to tell us?"

For the first time the man in the easy chair looked at him directly. His eyes held nothing. Andrew might have been just another part of the wall.

Harry Scott turned slowly to look at his brother. He said a whispered "Jack?" There was no answer, no reaction.

"You had no problem with alibi," Andrew said. "You set out from the clubhouse to do a solo round of golf. Nothing unusual for you. Near the parking lot, which is hidden by trees from the clubhouse, you dumped your bag and drove off. That was much less suspicious than having a firm alibi. Right?"

Still no answer. Tom Stamford said, "Any more of this stuff you've been holding back, Bailey?"

"Sorry about the minor suppression of evidence, Sergeant. Normally I would have come to you and stepped out of the picture. But I had a personal score to settle relating to old Jim. Also, you were a suspect."

Tom Stamford snapped, "*I* was?"

"Everyone was originally. But the field was narrowed by Jim Webber leaving what you could say was the killer's calling card."

"Whatever that means."

Andrew said, "Jim likened people to cards. I, for instance, was the ace of clubs. You and Jack Scott and Rennie were diamonds, the men aces. When Jack went there to kill Jim, the old man put out the ace of diamonds."

"Which could've been me or Jack."

"You were fully cleared tonight when the call was made to the reporter. Only Jack among the men was alone. He made the call from the old homestead."

The police officer nodded. He asked, "Anything else?"

"Only the gun," Andrew said. He turned again to Jack Scott. "I don't know if you still have the other revolver. I doubt if you kept it. You're not a fool. But it doesn't matter. What will be important is when Sergeant Stamford finds the store in the States where you bought the pair of guns. Its records will show, by serial number, which revolver was made out to you and which to Harry. The murder weapon is yours."

Andrew took a step back and leaned tiredly against the mantel. He and the others watched as Jack Scott moved. He moved slowly. He pulled himself forward, lifted his glass from the floor and got up. At a languid pace he went over to the bar. Leaving his glass there, he walked to the corner of the room which earlier he had found so interesting. He went down a ramp, opened a door, went from sight.

Starting to follow, Tom Stamford asked, "Where's that go to?"

Haig Wilson said, "Basement games room."

"Is there a way out?"

"No."

The police officer reached the door and tried the handle. He said, "It's locked."

From beyond the door came the sound of breaking glass. Tom Stamford snapped his head around. "I thought there was no way out."

Mrs. Maynard answered. She said, "That wasn't a window. It's the glass of the gun cabinet."

Everyone was silent; waiting; listening for the next sound.